'I joined your c[...]
not to become a [...]

'Have I asked you to b[...] he demanded.

'Not yet. And the day you do is the day I walk out. You've made it very clear what you want. Do you think I don't know what you're talking about?'

'What am I talking about?' he asked.

'You've said it again today: you think of me as "a kind of wife". But what you want is the wife without the marriage.'

He stared at her flushed face in silence for a moment. 'You've misunderstood,' he said brusquely. 'What I want is the marriage without the wife.'

MISTRESS TO A MILLIONAIRE

She's his in the bedroom—but he can't buy her love...

The ultimate fantasy becomes a reality

in

Mills & Boon® Modern Romance™

There'll be more chances to live the dream in future

Mistress to a Millionaire

titles, by your favourite authors

in your favourite series!

THE MILLIONAIRE
BOSS'S MISTRESS

BY
MADELEINE KER

MILLS & BOON®

All the characters in this book have no existence outside the imagination of the author, and have no relation whatsoever to anyone bearing the same name or names. They are not even distantly inspired by any individual known or unknown to the author, and all the incidents are pure invention.

First published in Great Britain 2004
Paperback edition 2005
Harlequin Mills & Boon Limited,
Eton House, 18-24 Paradise Road, Richmond, Surrey TW9 1SR

© Madeleine Ker 2004

ISBN 0 263 84125 1

Set in Times Roman 10½ on 11½ pt.
01-0205-50924

Printed and bound in Spain
by Litografia Rosés, S.A., Barcelona

CHAPTER ONE

SHE had never been so late in her life. And it wasn't even her fault.

As the airliner banked over the bay, Amy got a good look at the city where she had been expected hours ago. Many hours ago. She checked her watch. Yesterday, in fact.

The rising sun was slanting low over Hong Kong, making the millions of windows in the skyscrapers glow like gold. It was a breathtaking sight. With the thoroughness that marked everything she did, she had already studied the city in detail from guidebooks, and now, from several thousand feet up, she could pick out some of the major landmarks.

She did not have much time to practise her geography. It all swept past her window in a few seconds, the harbour, the Peak, Kowloon, the dense grid of streets that, even at this early hour of the day, already twinkled with innumerable cars.

She hunted urgently for the glass tower that was her destination. The plane was going fast. There it was! She managed to catch a glimpse of the tower, its hundreds of blue glass windows glowing in the morning sun. Then it was gone. But at least she had seen it. She was supposed to have been there, ready for her interview, at lunchtime yesterday.

Amy Worthington felt her stomach swoop in unison with the airliner's descent. She checked her watch. It was coming up for eight in the morning. Her interview with Anton Zell was history. So was the job it should have led to.

He would already be in another country. It had been made very clear to her that Mr Zell was only in Hong Kong for one day. And wherever he was, Anton Zell was not re-

5

nowned as a man who accepted excuses. She had been given her great chance and had missed it. It had been up to her to make sure she was present for the interview on time. For various reasons, she had chosen a flight that would have got her to Hong Kong with four hours to spare. Instead it had got her there eighteen hours late.

Had there ever been an unluckier flight? The misery had begun in London, as one delay after another to the flight had been announced; infinitely worse had been the pilot's laconic announcement that, due to engine trouble, they would be landing for repairs at an Asian airport whose name she couldn't even pronounce.

Amy felt like bursting into tears. This job was vitally important to her. It represented a quantum leap upwards. She knew she was capable of doing it, and doing it very well. It offered wonderful things—a spectacular salary, company accommodation in Hong Kong, travel, excitement.

But it also represented a major challenge. Whatever her capabilities were, she had not worked at this level before. She had everything—the intelligence, the confidence, the training—everything except the experience.

She needed to convince Anton Zell, known as one of the most demanding and powerful men in business, to give her a chance. And that meant persuading him to take a risk on her, an unknown, young and relatively inexperienced person, when there were many others, with a lifetime in industry behind them, who would also be queuing for this post.

Exactly how she was going to do that was a subject that had occupied her thoughts almost every hour of the past two weeks. Technically, she felt she knew the answers to almost any question Zell might throw at her. She had studied every scrap of information that had been released about his current projects and she had researched every possibility diligently.

She was adaptable and she felt ready to assimilate anything that might come her way.

That wasn't the problem.

The problem would be in persuading Anton Zell that someone of her youth was capable of standing up to the relentless pressures of the job.

The man who had helped to arrange this interview for her, her uncle Jeffrey Cookson, had put it succinctly: 'Zell moves at a pace that would burn most human beings to ashes. The interview is going to be hell, my dear. But get through it, and you'll be working in the next dimension.'

Nor was her physical appearance going to help. Her looks had often been described as 'angelic'. That, presumably, referred to her soft blonde hair and soft grey eyes, matched by fair skin and a sweet face. That there was more than a bit of devilry in her make-up did not appear on the surface. Nor did she look a month older than her twenty-eight years. Though her life had been no bed of roses, the sorrows and struggles she had been through had left no mark on her beauty. But there were occasions—and this was one of them—when she would have liked to look a little sterner and older.

She recalled the other thing Jeffrey had said. 'He's based in Hong Kong and does a lot of work all over south-east Asia. He'll have his pick of PAs who can speak the local languages. So you'll have to offer him something special, Amy.'

The jet engines roared deafeningly as the plane came in for landing at Kai Tak Airport. Staring out of the window, Amy saw the rooftops hurtling past, apparently only a hand's breadth beneath the wings. She had heard about this famously low landing approach, but she had never anticipated how stomach-churning it would be in real life!

She had no idea whether a Zell Corporation employee would be waiting to meet her. Perhaps they had given up on her. Her only hope—and it was a very faint one—was to see whether another interview could be arranged at short notice, somewhere else in the world. But it was a given that her failure had put her out of the running, and that Anton Zell had already appointed someone else to the job.

Getting from the plane to the terminal was a long shuffle along various claustrophobic, grey tunnels. It seemed interminable. Restlessly checking her watch, Amy saw that it was by now almost ten o' clock. On top of everything, she had probably also lost her hotel booking in this furiously busy city. She longed for a meal, a quiet room, a shower, and perhaps even an hour or two of sleep.

At last she retrieved her suitcase, which looked a lot more battered than it had done when she'd last seen it in London, and trudged through Customs to the arrivals hall, pushing her trolley ahead of her. As she emerged through the sliding doors she scanned the crowd anxiously, hoping to find a hospitable figure, perhaps holding up a sign with her name on it.

She did not seem to be in luck. A sea of faces stared back at her incuriously. Signs were being held up, but, since they were in Chinese, Arabic, Hindi and languages she did not even recognise, they only confused her.

She came to a standstill, hunting through the jumble for a single welcoming note. Impatient passengers jostled past her. She heard an exasperated comment in Chinese. A heavy trolley rammed painfully into her calves, making her gasp.

'You're blocking the exit.' The deep voice was accompanied by a strong hand which closed around her arm and pulled her inescapably forward. 'Lao Tzu said, "Swim against the current, but do not be a boulder in the stream".'

Amy looked up in bewilderment. The tall man who was hustling her away from the exit was wearing jeans and a dark blue silk shirt. But the lean, tanned face—the most handsome face in the world, according to a recent *Vogue*—was deeply familiar to her.

'Mr Zell?' she said in astonishment.

'Miss Worthington, I presume,' he replied laconically.

'Oh, I'm so sorry to be so late,' she panted, trying to keep up with his pace as he steered her through the crowds. 'My flight was delayed and then—'

'I know all about your flight,' he cut in. 'Take my advice and don't use that particular airline again. Their planes are old and they don't pay their ground crew enough.'

'I didn't expect you to meet me in person!'

'There's nobody *but* me, Worthington,' he retorted.

'I'm sorry?'

'It's Sunday morning,' he said. His strong hand was in the small of her back, pushing her relentlessly onward. 'I expect my staff to work hard six days a week. I don't ask anybody to work on a Sunday.'

'Oh, I'm so sorry,' she babbled. 'I really didn't mean to cause you so much inconvenience—'

'This is where we have to leave your trolley.' With effortless strength, he scooped up her bag and abandoned the trolley in his wake. 'Please don't get your coat caught in the escalator.'

She snatched her trailing coat up hastily as they got onto the escalator. 'Mr Zell, I do apologise for all this—'

He turned to her. His eyes were a deep cobalt blue. Their gaze hit her like a jolt of electricity. 'You have apologised four times now,' he said. 'Don't you think that's enough?'

'Yes, Mr Zell.'

'Then stop.'

'Yes, Mr Zell.'

She studied him covertly as the escalator rumbled upward. He looked formidably fit, broad-shouldered and flat-stomached in his casual silk shirt. And she thought she agreed with *Vogue*—he was probably the handsomest man in the world by a long way. His eyes and mouth were devastatingly sexy. He was in his early forties, and silver had appeared at his temples, but the rest of his hair, neatly cut—but not slicked back in approved zillionaire style—was black as jet.

Nor was there anything about his clothes that suggested he was fabulously wealthy and powerful. His watch was a steel sports model. No diamond glittered at his neat ears and his lean, tanned fingers were bare. The most expensive thing about him seemed to be his phone, a hi-tech titanium wafer into which he was now talking, telling his driver to meet them at the main entrance.

He snapped the phone shut, then turned to meet her eyes. 'Something wrong?'

'I—I understood you were only going to be in Hong Kong for a day. I hope you didn't have to change your plans on my account.'

'I'm planning to fly out to Sarawak this afternoon at two,' he replied. 'I'd like to get this interview over with.'

'Of course.'

'We're going to go to the office to do it.' He raked her with an up-and-down glance. She was suddenly acutely aware of the crumpled state of her clothes; her fawn trousers and jacket had been elegant when she'd set off, a lifetime ago. Now they proclaimed that she'd slept in them, woken in them, writhed in them, squirmed in them, wrestled a bear in them.

God alone knew what her hair looked like.

'I'm sorry, I'm not very smart for an interview!'

'I'll make allowances. Do you insist on changing? Want to go to your hotel?'

'Oh, I'm fine, thank you,' she said quickly. Her heart was pounding hard. She could not believe her luck. She was going to do the interview after all! She was getting a second chance!

'How about breakfast?'

'No, thank you, Mr Zell.'

'You're not hungry?'

'Breakfast is for wimps,' she said bravely.

'Many people consider me a monster,' he said curtly. 'Would you want to work for a monster, Worthington?'

'No, Mr Zell.'

'I am not a monster. If you are hungry or thirsty, please feel free to say so.'

'Well, actually—'

'Come.'

That powerful hand in the small of her back drove her out through the doors into the full, humid heat of a Hong Kong morning. A sleek black limousine nosed through the traffic and headed purposefully towards them. A chauffeur in a green uniform jumped out and hefted Amy's suitcase into the boot. Anton Zell propelled Amy into the interior.

The door thumped shut, cocooning her in a world of opulent luxury. Every surface was upholstered in cream leather and smelled delicious. She sank into her seat, blissfully feeling the air-conditioning starting to soak away the muggy heat.

Opposite her, Anton Zell was talking into his phone again. 'I'm running late, Lavinia,' he said in a clipped voice. 'A small but unavoidable calamity. I'll be in touch as soon as I can.'

The limo oozed out of the parking bay. 'To the office, Mr Zell?' the driver asked over his shoulder.

'Yes, Freddie. Stop at Choy Fat on the way.'

'Yes, sir.' The partition slid shut, sealing them in privacy.

Zell snapped his phone shut. His hands were strong and fine, she noticed. 'So what brings you to Hong Kong?' he demanded of Amy.

'I beg your pardon?'

'Why do you want this job?' His deep blue eyes were

piercing hers. The abrupt questions were unsettling her. She tried not to stare at him like a hypnotised rabbit.

'Is the interview starting now?' she asked.

'It started yesterday at noon,' he retorted. 'Aren't you happy at McCallum and Roe? Do you have some trouble there?'

'No, of course not.'

'"Of course not"? Then why have you flown all the way to Hong Kong to look for another job?'

'Because I'm capable of very much more than McCallum and Roe ask of me,' she replied.

'Does that mean you expect me to pay you very much more than McCallum and Roe pay you?'

'It means that I need a greater challenge in my work,' she rejoined. 'I'm not the sort of person who likes to coast along, doing the minimum. I like to be stretched. I need to feel that I'm always giving of my best. At the end of each week I want to look back and see that I've broken new ground, achieved things of substance—not just kept a chair warm.'

He watched her carefully as she spoke. 'Are you a risk-taker?'

The question flummoxed her for a moment. 'I am not a reckless person,' she replied slowly. 'But I am prepared to take risks when the reward seems worthwhile. And where what is risked is mine, and not someone else's.'

'You enjoy responsibility?'

'Yes,' she said candidly, 'I do.'

'Can you deliver projects on time?'

'Yes,' she said decisively.

'But you couldn't deliver yourself to this interview on time,' he pointed out silkily. 'You've arrived—' he checked his watch '—exactly nineteen hours late. You chose a flight that gave you too little margin for delays, Worthington. You took a risk. But what has been lost is mine, not yours. My time. People who take risks with my time do not last very long in my employment.'

'I understand,' she said in a low voice, stinging from the rebuke.

'Do you know why I need a new PA?'

'I have heard that your old PA had a sudden illness.'

'Marcie developed a heart murmur. She didn't tell me the full truth. She was trying to keep going until I found a replacement, but she collapsed,' he said. 'She only got out of hospital yesterday. Right now, I need someone urgently.'

Amy tried to smile. 'Well, here I am, Mr Zell.'

His answer was a grunt.

They had been driving along a freeway towards the stupendous collection of towers that was Kowloon. The driver now took an exit and entered a road that ran alongside the harbour. The blue water was crowded with boats, from huge cargo vessels to small shabby junks with their characteristic bat-wing sails. The quayside was strewn with piles of crates, coils of ropes, huge mountains of rusty chain and forests of multicoloured barrels. It was an exotic, chaotic world.

The limo pulled up at the kerb opposite a mooring where a large, dun-coloured houseboat was crowded in among smaller craft. On the congested deck, a family had set up a food stall and were serving a group of longshoremen. A smiling boy ran up to the car. Anton Zell slid the window down, letting in a fragrant smell of cooking.

'Boiled or crispy?' he asked Amy.

'I beg your pardon?'

'You wanted breakfast,' he replied patiently. 'In Hong Kong that means noodles. Do you like them slippery or fried?'

'Crispy,' she said determinedly, trying not to notice just how shabby-looking the junk was. It was probably unwise to look surprised at anything Mr Zell came up with, no matter how freakish. He gave the order to the boy, who scampered back to the boat.

'You come highly recommended by Jeffrey Cookson,' Anton Zell went on, studying her with his penetrating gaze. 'But then, he is your uncle.'

'He's been very kind to me,' she replied.

'So it seems. Apparently he brought you up after your parents died.'

'More or less.'

'So we should not be surprised that he thinks the world of you,' he concluded drily. 'But he is not the only one. Your first employers, Charteris Industries, gave you a glowing commendation, too.'

'I'm glad to hear that,' she said stolidly.

'So did McCallum and Roe. But people with glowing commendations are sometimes being hurried from job to job because they're unemployable.'

'That isn't the case with me,' she said.

The boy returned to the limo with two china bowls of noodles and two sets of chopsticks. Amy took the bowl gingerly. It was scaldingly hot. Praying she would not end up with strands of fried noodle hanging off her buttons, Amy dug the chopsticks into the food. It was surprisingly delicious.

'This is wonderful!' she exclaimed.

'These people are Hakka—boat people. They're good cooks. You looked as though you thought I was trying to poison you.'

'I thought it might be part of the stamina test,' she said innocently. 'Make the interviewee eat street food and see if she dies of dysentery.'

'You think you're too good to eat street food?' he asked, lifting one black eyebrow.

'Not at all,' she replied hastily. 'But in my experience

it's unusual for multimillionaires to eat breakfast with stevedores.'

'Nothing in life is free,' he replied calmly. She studied his face as he ate. All faces, in her experience, no matter how beautiful, had their weak points, angles from which they lost their beauty. But not Anton Zell's. No matter what angle you took, he was perfect. And the photographs had not even begun to show the vivid life that animated his expressions. 'But some of the best things are very cheap,' he went on. 'The food is good here and the view is wonderful.'

She had to agree. The view across the bay to the skyscraperscape on the opposite shore was magnificent. 'I'll remember that.'

'So you have already left McCallum and Roe?'

'I've been with them for four years. I never took any leave in that time. I had twelve weeks' accumulated leave built up. I asked if I could take that. It seemed an ideal way to go job-hunting.'

'Young Martin McCallum has something of a reputation with female colleagues.'

Amy felt her face flush. She swallowed a mouthful of crisp fried noodles. 'Yes, that's true.'

'Is that why you're so eager to leave?'

'No, it isn't, Mr Zell. And I resent that implication,' she added angrily.

His eyelids drooped slightly. 'You're a beautiful woman, young and single. Are you telling me that Martin McCallum failed to notice these things?'

'He noticed,' she said shortly. She had had her share of that particular problem. Female employees who had affairs with the boss's son and heir were not unknown. 'I have no problem keeping my private life and my job separate.'

'Did he make a pass at you?'

She was on the point of telling him that was none of his

business; but a glance at those dangerous eyes warned her not to avoid the issue. 'Yes, he did.'

'And how did you deal with it?'

'I told him I wasn't interested.'

'I hear that's not so easy.'

'I managed.'

'What would you do if I made a pass at you?'

She felt her stomach swoop, the way it had done in the plane coming in to land. His eyes were holding hers inexorably and she would have given anything to know the thoughts that lay behind them.

'I would turn you down, too,' she heard herself say.

For a moment there seemed to be a gleam of amusement in his eyes, but the passionate, deeply chiselled mouth did not smile. 'Why?'

'I told you, Mr Zell. Because I know how to keep my private life and my work separate.'

'What if the two were the same?'

'I don't understand.'

'Ever heard the expression "Sleeping your way to the top"?'

'If I thought you were that kind of man,' she said coldly, 'I would not have come all the way to Hong Kong for this job.'

'So what kind of man do you think I am?' he asked.

'I only know what I've heard.'

'And what is that?'

'That you're one of the most dynamic, creative men in your business. That working for you is an unparalleled opportunity to learn and grow. I know nothing about your private life, Mr Zell. That doesn't interest me.'

At last he broke the eye contact and finished off his noodles deftly. 'People on my personal team don't have a private life, Worthington. There isn't time or space for one. As my personal assistant, you'd be at my side for days at a time, weeks at a time, sometimes in very remote places. If you have a family, they will suffer. If you have a boyfriend, he will leave you. You will certainly learn and grow. But you won't have a private life.'

'Not even on Sundays?' she asked bravely.

'What?'

'At the airport you said you didn't expect your employees to work on Sundays.'

'You are not applying to become an employee,' he said. 'A personal assistant is not an *employee*.'

'What is she, then?'

He laughed softly and she saw that his white teeth were like everything about him—beautiful. 'You ought to know. You're applying for the job.'

'Well, I know that I'm to have no private life and no Sundays off. And your previous secretary was driven into the ground by overwork.'

'You're getting the picture. Now, let's see if we can build up a picture of *you*.' He rapped on the partition. 'To the office, Freddie.'

CHAPTER TWO

THE blue glass tower which she had glimpsed from the plane was infinitely more impressive from the ground. No logo was emblazoned on the exterior to proclaim that it was the headquarters of the man beside her, but its unique architecture had made it famous.

Freddie, the chauffeur, drove them down into an underground parking area beneath the building. Apart from uniformed security guards at the booms, the cavernous space was empty.

They got out at the brushed-steel doors of an elevator. Anton Zell entered a code on the key-pad and the doors opened. They went in, Anton carrying her bag. As the elevator whooshed upward, Amy felt her stomach dip for the third time that morning. A sense of unreality came over her. Whatever she had expected from this interview, the last thing she'd anticipated was spending a whole morning with Anton Zell himself!

They went right to the top floor and emerged from the elevator into a plushly carpeted reception area. This level, too, was eerily deserted. The doors to all offices stood open; in some, computer screens glowed and machines hummed, but not a human presence stirred. From this height, the views from the huge windows were astonishing, taking in the sprawling city below and the dazzling blue of the harbour.

Amy had expected he would lead her to his office. However, the room he led her into looked like the sickbay. Glass-fronted cabinets with medical supplies inside, a large double sink and a high steel couch completed the image of a doctor's surgery.

'Why are we here?' she asked.

'Your medical,' he replied succinctly. 'You signed the forms.'

Her jaw dropped. Of course she had signed the forms, agreeing to undergo a medical examination as part of the job interview—it was pretty much standard procedure for a job with this level of confidentiality.

'There's nobody here!'

'Except me. How observant of you.'

'*You're* going to do it?'

'Absolutely,' he said with a glint in his eye that might have been amusement.

'But—but that was supposed to be conducted by a doctor,' she gasped.

'By a Zell Corporation medical officer,' he corrected. 'Glynnis Prior. She's not a doctor, she's a nurse. And right now, our Glynnis is in Singapore, visiting her married daughter there. She was here yesterday—when you were supposed to arrive.'

'You're not qualified to do a medical on me!' she said, her face scarlet.

'I'm not going to give you a kidney transplant,' he said. 'Anyone with first-aid training can conduct the test. And I have plenty of first-aid training. I've done everything that's needed here many times. Of course, you can refuse to take the tests,' he added, watching her from under those formidable, dark eyebrows.

'And what would happen if I did refuse?'

'It would be taken as a sign of bad faith. That you have something to hide. The interview would end immediately and you would not be considered for the job.'

Grimly, she stared back at him. 'You mean—I would just go home?'

'At your earliest convenience.'

She thought furiously. She had not come all this way to back out now. But everything in her rebelled at the thought of letting Anton Zell perform a medical examination on her!

As if reading her thoughts, he picked up the blood-pressure cuff. 'None of it is a big deal, Worthington. Let's start with your blood pressure, shall we?'

Reluctantly, she rolled up her sleeve and sat on the couch. He wrapped the cuff around her arm and secured it. At the first sign of any funny business, she decided, she would walk out of here.

But where would she walk to? She was on the top floor of *his* building, all alone except for a bunch of *his* security guards, and no way back to the airport except in *his* limo, driven by *his* chauffeur.

He was already pumping up the cuff. She felt it bite into her arm. Listening carefully to the stethoscope pressed to her arm, he did not look like any doctor she had ever known.

'Do you speak Chinese?'

It was her weakest point and she tried not to wince. 'No, Mr Zell. I speak French and German and I can get by in Spanish and Italian.'

'Your blood pressure is a little high,' he commented, pulling off the Velcro cuff.

'I've been squashed up behind a family with young children on an airliner for twenty hours,' she retorted. 'And not much has happened since I got off to bring it down again!'

His fingers were biting into the sensitive inside of her wrist. 'And your pulse is rather fast, too.'

'Hardly surprising, either.'

'Any history of heart problems?'

'No,' she said.

'Do you suffer from high blood pressure? Hypertension?'

'No! Everything is usually normal. I'm suffering from the effects of a long flight, Mr Zell, nothing more.'

He noted the readings in a dossier. 'How did your parents die?'

Amy was looking out of the corners of her eyes to try and see how thick the dossier was, and what might be in it. 'My father died first,' she said. 'He had cancer. And no, before you ask, it wasn't a hereditary type. My mother nursed him to the end. But I think the experience shattered her. She was very frail. She died of pneumonia two years later.'

'How old were you?'

'I was eight when my mother died.'

He looked at her intently, but without any appearance of compassion. 'And this is when Uncle Jeffrey stepped in?'

'He was my mother's younger brother. He took me into his house. I grew up with his kids, my cousins.'

'And he put you through school?'

'Yes.'

'And then through college?'

'That's right.'

'Very altruistic of him.'

The suspicion of irony in his tone made her angry. 'Yes, it was, as a matter of fact. He wasn't very pleased to have an extra mouth to feed, but he did what he thought was his duty!'

He was washing his hands in the sink. Now he opened a sterile packet which contained some kind of kit. He pulled on latex gloves and began preparing a squat syringe. 'How did you repay your uncle's kindness?' he asked, watching what he was doing with narrowed eyes.

'I won scholarships all through school. And then all through college, too. What are you doing?'

'I'm going to take a blood sample,' he replied calmly. He probed the tender inside of her elbow with his fingertips and found the vein. 'Have any disabilities?' he asked, swabbing her skin with icy alcohol.

'No. Ouch!'

The needle slipped adroitly into her vein. The body of the syringe filled steadily with blood. She bit her lip. He was very close to her. She could feel the warmth of his skin, could smell a trace of some expensive cologne.

A sudden wave of perilous dizziness washed over her. She swayed, afraid she would fall.

'Am I hurting you?' he asked, steadying her with a strong hand.

'I'm fine.'

'You look pale. Does the sight of blood disturb you?'

'No. What is this blood sample for?'

'Well, it's the full moon, and I need a snack,' he replied. He slipped the needle out of her vein and pressed a pad of cotton wool to the spot. 'Hold that there for a moment, please. It'll be used for drug screening, Worthington. Do you use recreational drugs of any kind? Anything I should know about?'

'No!'

'Cigarettes?'

'No.'

'Alcohol?'

'A glass of wine now and then.'

'What sort of wine do you like?'

'Dry white, mostly.'

'Champagne?'

'Yes, very much.'

'I need you to sign this sample,' he said, giving her a pen. She wrote her name on the package and he put it in the fridge. 'The lab people will pick it up in an hour. Now I need a urine sample.'

'Well, you're not going to get one,' she said firmly.

'You don't have to do it here, you can go next door.'

'And you can go a lot further!'

He frowned. 'You're refusing to give a sample?'

'Yes, Mr Zell,' she said sweetly. 'I'm refusing to give a sample. You can take that as bad faith, good faith, or any kind of faith you choose. You've got my blood and that's as far as it goes.'

He sighed. 'Are you diabetic? Do you suffer from hepatitis?'

'No to both questions.'

'Then I suppose we can skip the urine sample.'

'Thank you.'

'You're very squeamish,' he said, writing in the dossier. 'If you're lucky—or unlucky—enough to land this job, you'll look back on this moment with a bitter laugh.'

'Thanks, I'll remember that.'

'OK,' he said, shutting the folder, 'we can continue the rest of this in my office. Let me put a plaster on that arm.'

He planted a small sticking plaster on the little red dot on her arm where his needle had gone in and led her down the corridor.

His headquarters were a corner office with magnificent views. Placed around the office were several scale models of recent Zell projects—complex masses of piping and tanks that made up the specialised oil refineries that he had pioneered and made his fortune out of. She recognised several of them—they were dotted all over the world, many here in south-east Asia.

Directing Amy to a chair, he opened an icebox and took out a champagne bottle and two frosted glasses. 'Is this what, in your experience, multimillionaires have for breakfast?' he asked.

'I suppose it's more traditional,' she said cautiously. 'Are we celebrating already?'

'No. But you look as though you could do with a drink. And you did say you loved champagne.' He poured the foaming Roederer into her glass. 'I thought you were going to pass out back there.'

'I did feel a momentary qualm,' she said. 'It was a long flight. A glass of Cristal might help, at that.'

'I need to ask you a few more questions,' he said, clinking his glass against hers.

'Of course.'

'Have you ever been arrested?'

She almost choked on her champagne. 'No.'

'Ever been convicted of any crimes or felonies?'

'No.'

'Can you tell me what the Laminate Plate System is?'

This time she did not stumble. 'LPS is a steel-elastomer-steel composite that Zell Corporation developed for building storage tanks. It's stronger and lighter than conventional steel. It's also much tougher, and that has obvious implications for marine construction. You've just leased the patent to a Korean shipbuilding company. If the system works out it may eventually earn you even more than you're currently making in the petrochemical industry.'

He was standing by the window, watching her over his glass of champagne. The morning light revealed the perfection of his figure—long, muscular legs, taut waist and powerful shoulders, supporting a neck and head that would have graced a Greek god. He seemed to smile slightly.

'You say the words ''petrochemical industry'' as though you really are fascinated by it.'

'I am,' she said. She indicated the scale models of refineries that stood around the office. 'I'm fascinated by complex engineering projects like these, Mr Zell. I like everything about your work. I especially like the environmental dimension you've started adding to everything you do. I like the care you take not to contaminate the ecologies where your refineries are located. I like the fact that you've used your brilliance to develop systems to refine used oil. Even your Laminate Plate System could have a beneficial impact on the environment. If it's used for the hulls of supertankers, oil spills from holes in the hull could become a thing of the past.'

'Commendably ecological sentiments,' he commented. He did not appear to have been flattered by her words; indeed, she had not been attempting to flatter him, only to express her genuine feelings.

'Yes, ecology matters to me,' she said. 'I want to hand something down to my children.'

'How many children do you have?' he asked blandly.

'None! It was a figure of speech.'

'Have you ever been married?'

'Never.'

'Do you have a current boyfriend?'

'I don't think that's relevant!'

'It's very relevant. I warned you, Worthington, your work schedule is not going to allow much in the way of a love-life over the next months. If you're in the throes of a great romance, planning a family some time soon, anything like that, then this is not the job for you.'

'I have nobody,' she said in a quiet voice. 'I'm not planning a family and there is no great romance in my life. I am happy to put the Zell Corporation first and foremost. Mr Zell, I may look young and flighty to you, but I can promise you that you won't find anyone more prepared to throw herself into this job than I am. I'm prepared to eat, drink and breathe Zell Corporation business from now on.'

He considered her from under brooding lids. 'You're starting to frighten me,' he said drily.

'I frighten myself sometimes,' she agreed. 'Would you like to hear about the greater vibration damping and improved thermal insulation offered by your new copolymer pipe linings? Or about how your unique solvent extraction system eliminates the need for thin-film evaporators as well as the costly hydrotreating step that makes your competitors' systems so expensive?'

'No, thank you.'

'Then perhaps I can tell you about the remarkable success Zell Corporation has had in the Marseilles plant, removing water, additives and contaminants at ambient conditions, so that the resulting oil can be handled with traditional distillation equipment?'

'All right, you've shown that you've done your homework and have a retentive memory.'

'I have an IQ in triple figures, too,' she said helpfully.

'I don't mean to patronise you,' he replied. 'Since Marcie's illness, I have been in desperate need of a new assistant. Look at this.' He tossed something into her lap. She picked it up. It was his slim titanium phone.

'Your cell-phone?'

'Satellite phone, Worthington. It works anywhere. I switched it to silent at the airport. Take a look at the screen.'

She obeyed and saw the blinking announcement: 37 missed calls, 44 new messages.

'I see your problem,' she said.

'Good. Do you want to start dealing with those?'

'Me? Now?'

'We don't have a lot of time. We're flying to Borneo at two.'

'"We"?'

'You and I. Us. We have a plant to inspect.'

'Does this mean I'm hired?' she said breathlessly.

'Unless your blood test shows you're a dope fiend or pregnant.'

'But I—I wouldn't know where to start!'

'For now, all I need you to do is answer that phone. Work out who is urgent and tell all the others I'm not available.' He indicated the huge teak desk in the corner of the office. 'That used to be Marcie's. When we get back to Hong Kong you'll start working out her systems. She won't be coming back to the office, but the secretaries will help you.'

'Mr Zell, I didn't expect to be starting work right now! I was planning to fly back to London tomorrow. If I'm really hired, I have things to arrange.'

'You've messed with my schedule. I think that gives me the right to mess with yours. I need you in Borneo this afternoon. When we get back, I'll make sure you have time to return to London and organise your life.'

'But I only packed clothing for three days!'

'What you're mainly going to need in Borneo,' he said succinctly, 'is a raincoat. It's the monsoon season.'

CHAPTER THREE

HUDDLED under the raincoat she had bought at Hong Kong Airport, Amy was still answering calls as they toured the Bandak refinery. It was late afternoon, but the wild weather made it almost as dark as night.

It was a panorama of rain in all its most turbulent manifestations—slashing down in curtains and beating on the buildings, driven up, down and sideways by the wind, pouring from the refinery's vast but as yet half-finished system of pipes in waterfalls, ploughing muddy torrents in the red dirt. Beyond the construction site, the jungle trees flailed wildly. Palm fronds and branches had broken off, and littered the earth.

The flight from Hong Kong, though made in Anton's private jet, had been rough, with lightning and high winds to contend with. The landing, at an airstrip near the construction site, had been hair-raising. On the ground, the rain, driven by gusts that were alternately warm and cool, was like nothing she had seen before. For the first time, she understood what the word *monsoon* meant. That sense of unreality washed over her again. She had not dreamed, as she flew into Hong Kong that morning, that by nightfall she would be in Borneo, Anton Zell's newest and rawest employee!

'We're ahead of schedule, despite the monsoon,' the site manager was telling Anton. She was listening to the conversation with one ear whilst taking a call with the other. They were standing with the engineers in the shelter of a cabin. The rain was pounding on the roof, a ferocious assault on all the senses. 'The first phase will come into production two months early.'

'Have the seals been tested?'

'They all hold up. The new system looks good.'

'What level of production are we looking at for phase one?'

'We've got the preliminary calculations here,' the man said, holding out a folder. 'We should be refining two thousand tons a month by next May.'

'Give those to my PA,' Anton commanded.

Amy accepted the folder from the site manager with a smile, never interrupting her conversation. She was already carrying a great wedge of information. And the woman to whom she was talking on the satellite phone was determined to speak to Anton, even though he had given her strict instructions that he was incommunicado.

'I'm so sorry,' she murmured, 'but Mr Zell is in a meeting and I cannot disturb him.'

'I can hear his voice, damn it,' the sharp, aristocratic voice snapped. She had identified herself as Lady Carron, and Amy was getting a vision of someone at the other end twirling an ebony cigarette-holder a foot long. 'Where is he? Propping up some bar, surrounded by floozies?'

'He's touring a refinery,' she replied evenly, 'and he's surrounded by engineers.'

'Who the hell are you, anyway? You're not Marcie.'

'That's correct. My name is Amy Worthington and I'm Marcie's replacement.'

'Well, what the hell has happened to Marcie?'

'Mr Zell worked her to death, Lady Carron. Can I take a message?'

'Yes, you damn well can. Tell Anton I will be waiting for his call.' The line clicked, but Amy was already taking the next call.

Anton came up to her and took her arm. 'We're just about

done here. The pilot says the weather is getting worse. I don't think it would be wise to try flying back to Hong Kong tonight.'

'I would rather be torn to pieces by piranhas.'

'Piranhas are South American, Worthington. We'll spend the night in a hotel in Kuching.'

'A Lady Carron keeps calling. She's expecting you to call back.'

'One of the more troublesome shareholders. We had our annual general meeting a couple of weeks back and she raised merry hell. She can wait. Let's get back to the Jeep.'

The road into Kuching was not so much a road as a shallow river. The Jeep made heavy progress, lurching in the thick mud. She relayed the other messages she had taken on his behalf. He seemed to listen with half his attention. Amy could see that his mind was still focused on the refinery with laser-like intensity, making calculations, projections, estimates.

They reached Kuching, a sprawling, picturesque town on the Sarawak River. Despite the monsoon, life was going on, and the streets were crowded. Everybody simply accepted the downpour.

The Jeep made its way through the evening traffic to the hotel, which was on the riverfront. It was a charming old place, full of old-world colonial glamour.

The room she was given had a balcony overlooking the river. She undressed, finding all her clothes, despite the raincoat, soaked through. She had a change of clothes in her bag—the outfit she had planned to wear for the interview. It was going to have to do.

The shower was modern and the water hot. She let it soak away the tiredness of the day. There had never been one like it in her life before. She had fixed on Anton Zell, the business genius, as a means to escape from England. But Anton Zell, the man, had entered her life like the monsoon itself, lifting her off her feet and blowing her thousands of miles off course. She wondered when—if ever—her feet were going to touch ground again.

She smoothed a cooling skin lotion all over herself, trying to convince herself that none of this was a wild dream. With a towel wrapped round her hair and another plastered round her torso, she emerged from the bathroom.

She stopped dead when she saw that Anton Zell was sitting on her bed, reading through the folders that the Bandak site manager had given them.

'Mr Zell!'

'Anton,' he said, not looking up. 'Nobody calls me Mr Zell. Is your first name really Amelia?'

'Amy.' She was acutely aware of how much of her nakedness was showing below and above the towel. 'And I'm not dressed yet.'

He glanced up and considered her with smouldering blue eyes. 'I've managed to shower and change and read twenty pages while you've been in there.'

'You're a man,' she said pointedly.

'A hungry man.' He was studying her legs unashamedly. 'I've booked a table at the restaurant.'

'I need to dress!'

He rose. Deliberately or otherwise, he brushed past her on his way out. 'You smell like a rainforest orchid. Perfumed and humid. Don't take all night, Amelia Worthington. I'll wait for you in the lobby.'

The dining-room was enchanting, a vast, high-vaulted room whose moulded ceiling was supported by ornate columns. It looked as though it had barely changed since the last century, with lovely old teak furniture and an eclectic collection of sofas and rattan chairs scattered around. The doors were open onto the garden to let in the breeze, though bamboo blinds had been lowered to keep out the worst of the monsoon rain. The tables were lit by candles. By their glowing light, the Iban masks and sculptures which hung on the walls seemed to take on a flickering life.

'None of those things are real shrunken heads, are they?' she asked Anton as they perused the menu.

He snorted. 'Go to the bottom of the class, Worthington. Shrunken heads are South American, like piranhas. The Iban take heads but they don't shrink them. Shrinking heads involves taking out the brain and—'

She interrupted hastily. 'All I want to know is, are they human?'

'I don't know. Some of them look familiar. That one is very like a personal assistant of mine who vanished a couple of years ago.'

'You enjoy tormenting me, don't you?'

'Yes,' he said frankly. 'There has been no head-hunting in Borneo for over half a century. That pretty cranium of yours is perfectly safe. I can recommend the curried fish. The mackerel is fresh and it's quite delicious.'

'All right,' she conceded. She was really too baffled by the strange words in the menu to make up her own mind. 'I love this hotel.'

'Good. I've stayed at the Hilton and the other smart hotels up-town, but this place is my favourite.'

'I hope I'm not letting you down. These clothes were meant for the interview, not going out.'

'Business, not pleasure?' He looked at her with smoky eyes. She was wearing the grey suit she had chosen for the interview, elegant, professional and formal. The feminine touch was supplied by the pearls that glowed against her pale skin. 'Who bought you those exquisite pearls?'

'They were my mother's,' she said, pleased that he had noticed. 'Aren't they pretty?'

'They're perfect for your wonderful complexion. Pearls and an English rose.'

She smiled. If he enjoyed teasing her, she enjoyed being

teased. It was a long time since she had felt this light-hearted. The rain was still pouring outside. Above them a fan rotated slowly, keeping the air cool. A waiter clad in snowy white except for his mustard-coloured turban took their order and then brought them the drinks they'd ordered.

'So,' Anton said, watching her with amusement in his eyes, 'whose idea was it to call you Amelia?'

'What's wrong with the name?'

'It's painfully Victorian. Amelia Worthington sounds like a virtuous orphan in Charles Dickens.'

'Well, I am an orphan,' she said lightly, 'though I don't know about virtuous.'

His expression changed. 'I forgot. I didn't mean to offend you.'

'No offence was taken. It happens to be an old family name. It was my great-grandmother's.'

'Oh, indeed.'

'Indeed.' She sipped her cocktail. He was such a hand-some man that just watching him filled her stomach with warm butterflies. It might be a lot harder than she had an-ticipated to be in close proximity with the best-looking man in the world, according to *Vogue*. 'In any case, you are an orphan too, aren't you?'

'Aha. Still showing me how well you did your home-work?'

'I'm just repeating what's written about you.'

His eyes were watching her mouth. 'Did you really tell Lavinia that I worked Marcie to death?'

'Lavinia?'

'Lavinia Hyde-White. Lady Carron.'

'Oh, the person who keeps calling? The one you de-scribed me to this morning as "a small but unavoidable calamity"?'

His devastating mouth quirked. 'Did I say that?'

'Yes, Mr Zell. And if you find Victorian names ridiculous, how about Lavinia Hyde-White?'

'Well, like yours, it's apparently an ancient family name.'

'Do you call her "Lavvy" for short?' she asked sweetly. 'Or perhaps just "Lav"?'

'It's always Lavinia.'

'I'm surprised you can keep a straight face at board meetings.'

'I invariably keep a straight face with rich and beautiful women.'

'Is that why you're laughing at me?' she retorted. 'Because I'm a poor, plain orphan?'

'You're not plain, Worthington,' he said, the expression in his eyes making her heart turn over. 'You have the face of…' He paused.

'Please don't say an angel. That would be so unoriginal.'

'Well, coming out of that bathroom in a skimpy towel, you looked like a very young angel who had been playing with an imp, and who'd had to have the brimstone scrubbed off her by the archangels.'

The cocktail had gone to her head and she couldn't help laughing. 'I know where the brimstone came from.'

'You have a lovely laugh,' he said. 'Original or drama school?'

'Don't be so cynical,' she retorted.

Their food arrived. As he'd promised, the curried fish was delicious, flavoured with coconut and ginger and other spices she'd never tasted before.

'I'm not an orphan in the sense that you are,' he said without preamble. 'I never knew my parents, so I did not have the experience of losing them, as you did. What you went through was much more traumatic.'

'It can't have been easy growing up in a series of foster homes,' she said.

He shrugged his broad shoulders. 'Most were good. A

few were very bad. I grew up in a lot of different environments and that made me the person I am. But going to live in someone else's house when you are young, with someone else's children, teaches you many things about life.'

'Yes, it does,' she said soberly.

'I guess that is something we have in common. Maybe your head won't end up on a spike after all. How's your fish?'

'It's wonderful, thank you. I'm glad I took your recommendation.'

'You'll need to be a good traveller in this job,' he said. 'Go any place, sleep anywhere, eat anything.'

'Anton,' she said, using his Christian name for the first time, 'I need to know something. Are you really giving me this job? Or did you just grab me because I was available, and can I expect to be dropped just as quickly when you're in a more serious mood?'

'Let's say that, like any job, there's a probationary period. If you measure up, you stay. If not, then you might be glad to leave anyway.'

'So I could be fired tomorrow? Well, at least there is a way out of your employment other than serious illness.'

'There's also death. Being fired is definitely worse than either of the other two.'

She toyed with her food, her small appetite already satiated by the spicy dish. 'And how will I know whether I'm measuring up?'

'You're asking me for a job description? Now, in the middle of Borneo?'

'Yes.'

He considered her carefully. 'Let me ask you, first. What do you think the principal part of your job is?'

She smiled. 'So far, it's been talking into that little titanium phone. You could replace me with an answering machine.'

'Let me explain some things about my working life. I don't spend much time in the office. Not any more. There was a phase of my life when I spent every waking hour at a computer or in a lab, designing systems to do the things I dreamed of. Now, I pay teams of people much cleverer than I am to do my research for me. I just come up with ideas. New ideas. As you know, this company is on the edge of a major new development based on technology I've been able to develop. But I am compelled to travel between my various projects. If they're being built, like the one we saw today, I make sure they're being built properly. If they're already running, like the one in Singapore that we're going to in five days' time, I make sure they're running properly. That's why I just warned you that you need to be a good traveller. You're never going to be home.'

'Nor are you,' she pointed out.

'Nor am I,' he agreed. 'I'm not married. I've always known that I could never inflict this kind of life on a wife. Not until I'm ready to settle down.'

'And when will that be?' she asked daringly.

'When I meet the right woman,' he said flatly. 'Until then, I'm married to my work. I have no space or time for women—the sort of women who want a commitment from a man. But no man is an island. Which is why I need a PA. And that brings me to the answer to the question I asked you a moment ago. The chief quality I look for in my personal assistants is companionship. Compatibility. Being able to amuse me and get along with me for long stretches of proximity. It's a very special kind of relationship. I hope you understand what I'm talking about.'

She drew back as though she had been burned and stared at him, feeling the food in her stomach start to curdle. 'Let me guess that Marcie was not grey-haired and seventy-ish?'

His languorous eyes widened at the change in her tone.

'What's the matter? You look as though you've seen a ghost—with a shrunken head.'

'Perhaps the curry disagreed with me,' she said shortly.

'I hope not. No, Marcie is not grey-haired and seventyish. She's in her thirties, tall and very elegant. In fact, she used to be a fashion model.'

'Lucky you.'

'I beg your pardon?'

'Unusual for a woman in her thirties to have heart problems.'

He was watching her pale face curiously. 'Yes,' he said curtly, 'very sad. It was a great shock.'

'Perhaps there were other complications,' she said, folding her napkin.

'What do you mean?'

Amy pushed back her chair. 'I'm really tired, Mr Zell. It's been a long day.'

He looked irritated, but did not argue. 'If you insist. I suppose we should hit the hay. Let's go upstairs.' He rose from the table with her. They walked out of the dining-room. The Iban masks on the walls seemed to be leering at her mockingly as she left.

On the landing outside her room, exhaustion washed over her. The blood seemed to drain from her heart and she staggered. Anton caught her arm to support her.

'What's wrong with you?' he asked suspiciously.

'It's been a long day,' she said with an effort. 'I just need sleep.'

He reached out and hooked one finger around the string of pearls that hung at her throat. His eyes were locked on hers. He drew her face to his. At the last moment, she closed her eyes involuntarily.

She felt his warm lips touch hers, a contact so sweet, so intimate, so achingly familiar.

So dangerous.

She looked up into his eyes. They were dark and intent. He took the key from her nerveless fingers and opened her door.

'Goodnight,' he said. 'Mind the head-hunters don't bite.'

She shut the door and locked it as though the devil himself were on the other side.

Amy was awakened very early the next morning by thunder.

She opened her eyes slowly, remembering where she was. Up in the vaulted ceiling, a fan chopped at the air languidly. She took in the elegant room lit by a rainy dawn. Yesterday was like a dream to her. It was hard to believe it had all happened. Yet there was a heavy stone in her chest that told her that her heart remembered, even if her mind didn't.

Her lips felt swollen, as though that momentary kiss had seared her mouth, leaving the tender skin burned.

Fragments of yesterday echoed in her mind. *Ever heard the expression 'Sleeping your way to the top'?* That was what he had asked her at the harbour in Hong Kong. *It's a very special kind of relationship. I hope you understand what I'm talking about.*

Oh, yes.

She knew exactly what he was talking about. He had made it very clear. A wealthy man with no wife, married to his work, always on the move. No space or time for women—*the sort of women who want a commitment from a man.* But no man was an island, he had said. That was plain enough.

Thunder muttered overhead. Amy rose and went out onto the balcony, wrapping the sarong around herself that the hotel had provided.

Young Martin McCallum has something of a reputation with female colleagues. When Anton had said that yesterday, her heart had nearly stopped; why hadn't she seen that as the glaring clue it was? Had he heard? Did he know what had happened to her at McCallum and Roe? Was that why he'd thrown the job at her so casually—because he needed someone in Borneo, and knew that she had a *reputation*, too?

The grey-green river swept in a curve past the hotel. Already, though it was just after dawn, the river traffic was building up, sampans and barges drifting through the sheets of rain. She stared at the boats unseeingly. She had wanted so desperately to be out of England; well, here she was, about as far from London as you could get in every way.

Lightning glared, and thunder crashed overhead. Had she really been so dim-witted as to leap from the frying-pan into the fire? How could she be so *stupid*? What had been the point of travelling thousands of miles, just to meet another Martin McCallum? Hadn't she learned her lesson? Hadn't she been through enough pain yet?

In London she had felt that everyone was staring at her, that everyone *knew*. Knew how foolish she had been. Knew that she had been naïve enough to allow herself to be seduced by the most notorious womaniser in the City. Knew that she had allowed herself to be blinded by his promises and dazzled by his charm.

That she hadn't even noticed when they'd all been laughing at her, as she walked around with starry eyes.

That she hadn't taken, hadn't even *understood*, the warnings.

That she'd been so impossibly stupid that, when she'd learned she was pregnant, she'd expected Martin McCallum to be as delighted as she was.

Her eyes blurred with tears as she remembered that terrible day, Martin's mockery turning to fury as he heard her stammering declaration that she wanted to have the baby, wanted the child that had been conceived, so she still thought, out of their love. Martin shouting at her, asking her just how stupid she was. Martin telling her there had been no love, only sex. Martin screaming at her to do something fast.

Do something, you little fool. I'll pay.

Do what, Martin?

What do you think, for heaven's sake? Open your eyes! Get rid of it. Or I warn you, you're on your own. I'll get my father to sack you and you can see how you like being an unemployed single mother!

Amy huddled into her sarong. She had certainly opened her eyes that day. Her illusions had evaporated like wraiths.

And with them had also gone her heart and her soul. Her happiness, her self-respect, her sense of wholeness, her feeling that life was good and that she was good and that her happy future was unfolding.

And that, of course, was why she had found herself here in Borneo, standing alone on a balcony, looking at the dark green jungle. Like a creature on the very edge of civilisation, not sure whether it belonged to the light or to the darkness.

It had taken her so long to recover from the psychological effects and start to believe in herself again. She'd fixed so much hope on Anton Zell. Zell, the genius, the billionaire who cared, the oil-industry captain who protected the environment, the decent human being, the beacon of hope.

If he turned out to be another abuser, who thought a fat salary paid for her body in his bed, then the world was indeed a bleak place.

She could hear tapping at her door. She wiped the tears from her face and went to answer it.

It was Anton. He was already dressed. She had forgotten how handsome he was; his deep blue eyes jolted her.

'I'm glad you're up. We need to make an early start.'

'OK.'

'Make me a cup of coffee, Worthington. The kettle in my room is broken.'

'Of course.' She let him in and fumbled with the coffee things.

'Have you been crying?' he asked.

'It's just rain,' she said, her back to him. 'I've been standing on the balcony. The view is really something. I didn't see it last night, it was dark and—'

He touched her sarong. 'You're soaked! What were you thinking of?' His strong hands closed around her shoulders and drew her round to face him. He looked down into her face. 'Amy, what is wrong with you? Are you ill?'

'I'm fine,' she said. She tried to sound brave, but she was trembling in his grip.

'Is there something you want to tell me?' he asked quietly. 'Something I should know?'

She managed to laugh. 'Oh, no. I think I got a tummy bug yesterday and I didn't sleep very well, that's all. It's over now. Do I look that bad?'

He seemed unsatisfied with her prevarication. 'Don't hide things from me, Worthington. Don't even try. I assure you that I will find out every single thing about you in the end. So if there's something to say, say it now.'

'There's n-nothing!' she stammered.

'What happened last night? One minute we were having fun, the next you were running for cover. What went wrong? Was it something I said?'

Amy took a deep breath. Just looking into that face made her heart pound like a trip hammer. He was a very suspicious man—and a frighteningly perceptive one. She tried hard to give him a more genuine smile. 'No. It was just the bug. Sometimes these things require a fast exit.'

He nodded. 'All right, if you say so. At least you look more like yourself again. Bright-eyed and bushy-tailed.'

'I don't have a tail.'

'You have bright eyes. Usually. They're a lovely shade of grey, but sometimes they go absolutely black.'

'Do they?' she said with a breathless laugh.

'Yes. Then you stop looking like an angel and start look-ing like a creature from the other place. Still beautiful—but darkly beautiful, not brightly beautiful.'

'Let me make your coffee,' she said, breaking away from the moment in panic. She fussed with the spoons busily. Her heart had lifted for a moment but now it was hard and heavy again. The sense of nightmare was back. Someone else had said things like that to her. Things that made her spirits soar and joy rise in her.

Someone called Martin McCallum.

CHAPTER FOUR

THE job had been offered with 'accommodation in Hong Kong', but that had hardly described the Causeway Bay flat Anton had installed her in.

A fully serviced apartment, decorated in the height of style, equipped with the latest sound and viewing systems, with wonderful views of the bay, close to the most glamorous shopping and possessing—luxury of luxuries in crowded Hong Kong—its own private balcony, it was the most beautiful 'accommodation' Amy had ever been in. Judging by her boss's laid-back style, she doubted whether Anton Zell himself lived in anything more thrilling.

You couldn't even accuse the apartment of being soulless, like most corporate accommodation, because the gleaming Oriental antiques with which it had been furnished exhaled the very mystery of ancient China.

The only problem was that she'd had so little chance to spend time here that, after three whole months, she still didn't know how everything worked.

Taking the initial decision to accept the job had been hard. She'd felt as though she were between the devil and the deep blue sea. The memory of that kiss had almost kept her in London. To tell the truth, it had been a chance meeting with a former colleague from McCallum and Roe that had decided her. The look in his eyes, knowing and somehow smirking, had reminded her that there was nothing left for her in London.

Whereas here in Hong Kong…

She threw the glass doors open and walked out onto her balcony with a glass of freshly squeezed orange juice. The bay was as blue as a sapphire, as blue as Anton Zell's eyes. In the typhoon harbour below her apartment, the luxury yachts of the very rich swayed gracefully alongside the picturesque junks of the boat people, where barefoot children scampered and women hunkered down beside kerosene stoves on the deck.

The great forest of glass towers was backed by a mountainscape of brilliant white cloud, building up into a cobalt sky. It was Sunday morning and she wasn't due back at the office till eight o'clock Monday morning. In the past three months she had worked right through every weekend. That had included almost a whole fraught month in Singapore to visit a refinery which was not meeting production targets due to various system malfunctions.

Solving the problems had taken a sustained effort. She had never seen anyone work as hard, or with such concentration, as Anton had during that month. If there were any doubts in her mind as to exactly how he had become so successful, they had been removed forever in Singapore. He was able to concentrate his mind like a laser, cutting relentlessly through problems until a solution was found.

She had been at his side constantly, relaying instructions, taking calls, scheduling his appointments. But whether she had offered him the companionship, that *special relationship* that he had spoken of, she could not tell; every waking hour had been spent in work and neither of them had had much energy to do anything than grab a bite of food and go to sleep in their hotel when the day was over.

There had been no repetition of that kiss in Borneo, though it continued to haunt her memory like the touch of a jungle flower. What was the phrase he had used? A rainforest orchid, perfumed and humid. That was how the touch of his lips on hers stayed in her mind, something exotic and definitely dangerous.

She shook the thought away. Remembering the way he

had kissed her in Borneo brought back other things, things that darkened her day.

Such as the details she had learned about Marcie, her predecessor, from Glynnis Prior, the pleasant, middle-aged medical officer who had been so happy to talk to her when she'd gone into the sickbay for a plaster to put on a cut finger.

And it was a Sunday and she had leisure to explore this wonderful new world she was in. She did not want to think about Anton Zell and his dark mysteries. The trouble was, she hardly knew where to begin. She drank her juice, watching the sails drift across the busy harbour.

The door buzzer sounded. Wondering who it could be—the building had a strict policy of keeping out hawkers—she went to the entryphone. The figure on the closed-circuit television screen was awfully familiar.

'Anton?' she said, snatching up the phone.

He was standing with his hands in his jacket pockets. 'Are you going to keep me waiting on the street?'

'I'm trying to let you in!' She was frantically hunting for the right button to open the door. She'd never had to let anyone in before! It had to be this one with the red key on it. She pressed it and was relieved to see Anton's impatient figure disappear from the screen.

She ran to the bathroom, her heart beating fast, to try and make herself presentable for this unexpected call. She just had time to brush her hair into shape when the doorbell chimed. Slightly breathless with her haste, she opened it.

Anton walked in. Her efforts to beautify herself were wasted; he hardly spared a glance on her, but looked around the apartment with piercing eyes. 'Damn, I'd forgotten how nice these apartments are.'

'It's beautiful. I'm very happy here.'

'You ought to be,' he said drily. 'You live better than I do. I have a bachelor flat in Wanchai.' He shrugged. 'Oh, well, I can get to work in fifteen minutes. So—are you settling in?'

'I've hardly had a chance to find my feet,' she said with a smile. 'The driver picks me up every morning, but I still haven't really seen anything of Hong Kong!'

'That's why I dropped by,' he said. 'I need to do some things around town. You could tag along and get an eclectic guided tour.'

'You mean—come with you?' she asked hesitantly.

He gave her a dangerously lifted eyebrow. 'Since we've spent the last three months in each other's pockets, I guess the prospect of yet another day in my company is hardly appealing?'

'No, it's not that!'

'If I promise not to mention light end stripping, surge vessels or vacuum distillation, would that help?'

She smiled. 'Actually, I find engineering details fascinating.'

'I see. It's just me you find repulsive?'

Amy gave in. 'I'll get a raincoat.'

'Ah. You're turning into an old China hand.'

The flimsy raincoat, which could be squeezed into a pocket, went with her everywhere; she had learned early about the vagaries of Hong Kong weather, no matter how brightly the sun shone. It was April, a lovely month in Hong Kong, but that did not rule out rain.

There was no limo today; Anton's car, a sleek black two-seater, was parked outside.

'Wow,' she said admiringly, 'nice wheels!'

'Well, get in.' He opened the door for her. His hand in the small of her back propelled her in. She had never quite got used to that strong hand which gave her those unanticipated shoves in the right direction.

'Fast and furious, but no room for baggage,' she said, settling into the bucket seat. 'Like her owner.'

He switched on the engine with a throaty rumble and set off. The top was down and it was fun to feel the wind blowing her hair. She settled back, feeling absurdly excited.

'Why did you say that?' he asked after a silence.

She glanced at him. 'What?'

'That I had no room for baggage.'

'Oh, I'm sorry, I didn't mean to be cheeky.' His expression was serious and she was afraid she had offended him. 'It wasn't meant to be a negative comment. Just that—'

'That?'

'Well, it's your style. No prisoners, no passengers and no Sundays off. It's a nice way to live if you have nobody else to consider.'

'And nobody else to consider you.'

'Anton, you are the centre of a whole universe of people who think the sun rises and sets with you. Of course people consider you. They rejoice in your smile and tremble at your frown.'

'More the latter than the former, I think.'

'You should smile more often.'

'I'm smiling now,' he said, baring his teeth like a tiger.

'And I'm rejoicing,' she said. 'Look.' She grimaced back.

'I *am* human,' he said. 'I'll even treat you to breakfast.'

'As long as it isn't noodles. I've tried every combination of noodle for breakfast since I've been here, and I still crave a plain old English fry-up.'

'That can be arranged,' he said. 'I even know where to get English bacon and eggs in this town. I know every restaurant in Hong Kong. I eat out three times a day. What I never do is sit down at my own table to eat a meal made in my own kitchen.'

'Stop, you're breaking my heart,' she said. 'I know how you dream of a wife in curlers, frying you liver and onions, while your three kids tug at your sleeve yelling, "Daddy, Daddy"!'

'Hmm, that does sound awful.'

'Oh, please. With your two-seater sports car and your bachelor apartment? Working till midnight then slurping noodles and whisky in some Wanchai strip club? Everything about you screams ''single and loving it''.'

'And you?'

'What about me?' she laughed.

'You're working for the single-and-loving-it guy. When you came to me for the interview, you told me there was nobody more prepared to throw herself into the job than you. You said you wanted to eat, drink and breathe Zell Corporation business from now on.'

'Yes, I did. And I am.'

'So what's the difference between you and me?'

'Maybe none, at that. Except I don't complain about it. I'm an obsessive-compulsive loner and happy with it.'

Anton grinned. 'You're only half joking, aren't you?'

'I just think neither of us is ever going to be sitting at that homey table with the three kids and the fried liver and onions. So it's pointless to dream about it.'

'It's never pointless to dream.'

The conversation was quickly getting painful for her, so she changed the subject. 'Where are we going, anyway?'

'Battery Street. I thought you might like to see the jade market.'

'Jewellery? Oh, yummy. Now you're talking.'

'Jade is more than just jewellery, Worthington,' he warned. 'Jade is a way of life. It's the stone of heaven. It's a medicine, a religion, an art form. You rub it for health and worship it for its beauty and take it into the next world. You can even eat it if you want to live for ever.'

'No, thanks. Four score years and ten contain trouble enough. Anything else I should know?'

'Well, many kinds of stone go under the name of jade, and it can be green, white, lavender, red, yellow or even black. But the two most important stones are nephrite and jadeite. Nephrite is by far the most common. Jadeite is harder and more valuable.'

'Which should I buy?'

'Buy whatever speaks to your heart.'

'Am I going to be robbed?'

'Depends if you follow my advice.'

The market, at the corner of Kansu and Battery Street, was crowded and busy. As they strolled, Amy watched, fascinated, as small groups of men, some of them ancient enough to sport long white Confucian beards, haggled over paper packets of the green stone.

The covered part of the market was crammed full of booths and stalls. As Anton had predicted, a bewildering assortment of goods was on offer. There were man-sized boulders of raw green jade; boxes of tiny beads and blobs; carved animals both great and small, realistic and mythical. There was jade of every colour imaginable, from deepest black to snow-white, taking in the hues of the rainbow between.

Threading their way through the crowds, they were assailed by tradesmen offering them jade of every description, extolling the quality, calling on them to admire the colour, holding pieces aloft to demonstrate the transparency. Much of it was astonishingly beautiful to Amy's eyes.

One shop in particular caught her fancy. The owner had arranged a multitude of small carved animals on shelves. Looking closely, she marvelled at the dragons and lions.

'These are beautiful!' she called to Anton. 'And they look really old!'

He joined her, looking at the collection with a critical eye. 'Some of them are genuine,' he said. 'Anything that's claimed to be over a hundred and fifty years old is likely to be a reproduction. But these late Qing Dynasty ones are authentic. They date from the nineteenth century. See how polished they are? They've been lovingly cherished over generations.'

'I adore this piglet,' she said, picking up the fat little creature and admiring its chubby cheeks and pop eyes.

The shopkeeper came forward. 'Beautiful piece,' he enthused. 'Five hundred dollars.'

Amy blenched at the price. 'Too much for me,' she said, putting it hastily back.

'Wrong animal, in any case,' Anton said. 'These animals correspond with the Chinese astrological zodiac. You, unfortunately, were not born a pig.'

'What am I, then?' she demanded.

'It gives me great pleasure to inform you that you are a monkey,' he said gravely. 'This one would be more appropriate.'

She took the carving he was holding out to her, and fell in love instantly. The little monkey was clutching a fruit to its chest with both arms and looking over its shoulder anxiously to see if there was any competition for the delicacy. It was so exquisite that she gasped out loud. 'Oh, what an adorable monkey! I love it!'

Anton's eyes narrowed angrily. 'You've just doubled the price, damn it,' he growled.

'I don't care,' she hissed back. 'What are the monkey's qualities?'

'Well, if you had been born a pig, you would have been a much nicer person to know and I would not have hesitated about employing you.'

'I didn't notice you hesitating about employing me,' she pointed out.

'But as a monkey,' he went on, ignoring the interruption, 'I benefit from your superior intelligence and charm. Though your deep distrust of other people makes you hard to get close to.'

'You're making this up! And what are *you*? A tiger, I suppose?'

'A dragon.'

'Oh, now, why am I not surprised to hear that? And what are your qualities, oh, great dragon?'

'I'm a brilliant perfectionist who makes impossible demands on others.'

'That's frightening,' she said. 'There's something in this astrology stuff after all.'

She let Anton take over the haggling and eventually bought the delightful little monkey for a third of its initial price. Although, as Anton told her sternly as they walked out, it would have gone down even further if she hadn't shown such conspicuous signs of being infatuated with it.

'I'll know better next time,' she said. But she couldn't have been more pleased with her purchase. She unwrapped it and crooned over it happily. 'I suppose I should have asked whether it's nephrite or jadeite.'

'It's nephrite,' Anton said. 'The carving is fine, but the stone isn't particularly valuable. Come, I want to show you something special.'

He took her arm possessively in his strong hand and led her down a dark alleyway where the shops were less crowded and there were no tourists to be seen. At the very end of the lane was a shop with a carved red door. It appeared to be closed but when Anton rapped at the dragon-shaped wrought-iron knocker, it was opened by an elderly man wearing spectacles with flip-up magnifiers on each lens. He greeted them warmly.

'Mr Wu,' Anton said, 'I was hoping you could show us some of your wares.'

'Of course,' the old man said, opening the door wide. Again, Amy was aware of that strong, forceful hand in the small of her back, urging her forward.

Mr Wu ushered them courteously to chairs. 'Please, sit down. Some tea?'

'That would be very nice,' Anton said.

Amy sat beside him in front of the desk where the old man had been sorting through a collection of ancient fragments that looked like dull stone coins, some with holes drilled in them. 'Those are *bi*,' Anton murmured in her ear. 'Religious objects from China's distant past.'

'How old are they?' she whispered back.

'Shang Dynasty,' he answered. 'From the sixteenth century.'

'Wow, five centuries old!'

'No,' he said patiently, 'the sixteenth century BC. They're *thirty-seven* centuries old. The Shang Dynasty corresponds to our late Stone Age.'

'Oh,' she said.

'China is a very ancient civilisation,' he said, deadpan.

Mr Wu came back into the room with a tray. He served them tea in small cups, and, while they sipped the scalding, chrysanthemum-scented brew, began unfolding a carefully wrapped baize bundle.

Amy watched in fascination. The baize roll contained around a dozen pockets, and from each pocket Mr Wu extracted a piece of jade. There were rings, earrings, bangles and necklaces of polished beads. The workmanship was perfect, yet extremely simple. What made her gasp was the colour of the stone—a deep, almost iridescent green that she had never seen in her life before. The pieces glowed with an intensity that was alive. For the first time she believed Anton's tales of how jade was revered and regarded as the stone of heaven.

'There's nothing like this anywhere in the market,' she said in awe. 'I've never seen such an electric green!'

'Burmese imperial jade,' Mr Wu said, beaming. 'As beautiful as emerald!'

'Yes, it is,' she agreed. 'Most of the emeralds I've seen don't begin to match this for beauty. These beads are wonderful. And these rings…I think I would rather have one of these than an emerald.'

'What about this piece?' Mr Wu said gently. He was holding out a bangle. 'This material is the finest quality. And the workmanship is equal to the material.'

She took the bangle. The stone was cool, despite the warmth of the shop. It was, as Mr Wu had said, the best piece in the collection; the stone was a deep and vivid green. It had been carved with a dragon, whose sinuous and muscular body writhed all around the band, his fire-breathing jaws meeting his fiery tail.

'It's marvellous,' she sighed, turning it in her fingers so that the dragon seemed to twist as though alive, his scales shimmering. The thing was so beautiful that she was almost reluctant to hand it back to Mr Wu.

'Try it on,' Anton suggested. She slipped her hand into the cool green hoop. Against her pale skin, it looked wonderful. When she began, reluctantly, to take it off again, he shook his head. 'Keep it on.'

'I might get attached to something like this,' she said with a smile.

'I hope so,' he replied.

'What do you mean?'

Mr Wu rose. 'I will prepare more tea,' the Chinese man said courteously, and disappeared into the back of the shop, leaving them alone.

Anton looked her in the eyes. 'This is yours,' he said.

Amy's heart sank swiftly. 'Oh, no! This is a very valuable piece!'

'It is yours.'

Her face reddening, Amy shook her head. If this was his idea of a joke, it was a highly embarrassing one. She pulled the jade bangle off her wrist. 'Anton, I can't accept this.'

'It's a gift,' he said. 'A way of welcoming you to the Zell Corporation and wishing you luck in your new job.'

'Those are very nice sentiments,' she said awkwardly. 'Nevertheless, I can't take this. Please give it back to Mr Wu.'

Anton's eyes were cool. 'I can't. I've already paid for it. And it does seem to have your name on it.'

She looked at the bangle closely. Its section was in a D-shape. On the smooth inner surface of the jade, Chinese characters had been exquisitely incised.

There were also some words in Roman characters: the date, and the inscription, To Amy from Anton.

She was dumbstruck for a moment. 'You've had it engraved!'

'I knew you were going to like it,' he said, as though there had never been any other option. 'I knew it would suit you perfectly, and it does. I want you to wear it to the office.'

Amy's whole body felt hot and flushed. She had a sensation of panic, of being suffocated in this small, ornate shop with its drawers full of treasures. 'You don't understand,' she said urgently. 'I *cannot* accept this gift, beautiful as it is. Please ask the jeweller if he can polish this inscription out.'

'That's impossible. It's been cut too deep.' He was clearly getting impatient. 'What is the matter, Amy? I don't understand you.'

'Then try,' she begged him urgently. 'New employees don't accept lavish gifts from their employers. I'm not a fool. I know what this bangle must be worth.'

'Amy,' he said shortly, 'I can afford to buy you a piece of jade.'

'The point is not what it means to *you*,' she said, her eyes flashing angrily at his intransigence, 'but what it means to *me*! It would put me under intolerable pressure.'

'Why are you spoiling my day?' he asked, frowning at her.

'You're spoiling *my* day, Anton. Everything was lovely up until now—the drive, the market, helping me choose that little monkey—but this is just awful!'

'You think the bangle is awful?'

'Of course not. It would be a fabulous gift from a man to his wife, but not between employer and employee!'

He shrugged, growing colder as she grew hotter. 'I think of you as a kind of wife, Worthington,' he said with ironic mockery.

'Then stop thinking of me like that,' she retorted.

'I don't understand what the hell is eating you,' he said, his eyes growing cold. 'It's just a gift.'

'Putting thousands of dollars on my arm is not "just a gift". I joined your company to work, not to become a concubine.'

'Have I asked you to be that?' he demanded.

'Not yet. And the day you do is the day I walk out, Anton. You made it very clear what you wanted in Borneo—and you've been dropping subtle hints all morning, about how lonely and neglected you are. Do you think I don't know what you're talking about?'

'What am I talking about?' he asked.

'You've said it again today: "a kind of wife". But what you want is the wife without the marriage.'

He stared at her flushed face in silence for a moment. 'You've misunderstood,' he said brusquely. 'What I want is the marriage without the wife.'

'It's the same thing,' she retorted. 'You're very adept at solving problems, and this is your solution to one particular problem.'

'If I wanted sex,' he said grimly, 'I would get it at those Wanchai strip clubs where you say I slurp noodles and whisky till dawn.'

'I know you go there, because you've thrown the tabs at me to pay the next morning. Whatever you're slurping there does not come cheap!'

Anger made his eyes darken. He took the jade bangle from her and dropped it into his pocket. This time, the hand in the small of her back was almost rough. 'All right, that's enough. Let's go.'

CHAPTER FIVE

SHE felt achingly sick as they drove back to Causeway Bay in silence. She knew she had said things back there in Mr Wu's shop that she should not have allowed to pass her lips. She would be lucky to keep her job.

If he only knew the raw nerve he had touched—that he kept on touching, with almost every thing he did or said. There were moments when a kind of madness took her over and filled her with unbearable anguish.

True to form, the moist banks of white clouds had closed in swiftly and by the time they reached her apartment block, the rain was pouring down, making pedestrians dash to and fro, buried under umbrellas or plastic wraps. Of course, all Anton had to do was touch a button on the dashboard and the hood of the sports car closed over them with an electric whirr. Men like Anton did not get wet when it rained.

He pulled up outside her place. The rain drummed on the canvas hood over their heads. He turned to her with sombre eyes.

'Maybe you can give me an explanation before you go?'

Her throat was tight. 'Anton, I'm sorry I spoke out of turn today. I had no right to say some of those things. But I felt I had to say them. I don't want you to get the wrong impression about me.'

'And what impression would that be?'

She stared out at the rainy forest of masts, unable to meet his eyes. 'Personal assistants find out all sorts of things. It's the nature of the job. You know—like a wife without the marriage.'

'What things?'

'My predecessor. The beautiful Marcie. You told me she had a heart murmur and had to leave suddenly.'

'And?'

'Marcie had a medical check-up three days before she left so suddenly. Whatever the report said, there was nothing wrong with her heart.'

'You've looked in her file?' he asked in a dangerous voice.

'No, of course not. Somebody told me.'

'Who told you?'

'It doesn't matter. Lots of people are speculating about Marcie and her heart murmur. But she's not in Hong Kong any more. She was whisked away to a clinic in Switzerland.' She faced him, her mouth twisted in a painful smile. 'There was *some* kind of medical emergency. Something that had to be dealt with urgently. But it wasn't a heart murmur.'

'Why should this concern you?' he growled.

'Why?' She extended one finger. 'Firstly, because she was my predecessor. Secondly, because you lied to me about why she left. Thirdly, because she didn't leave on health grounds—her contract was terminated because you fired her.' She held up three fingers for a moment, then let her hand drop back into her lap. 'That's why it concerns me.'

'I see,' he said heavily.

'Wherever Marcie is now,' she said in a pain-filled voice, 'I don't want to end up in the same place.'

'I hope you won't,' he replied.

'I'm alone in this life, Anton. I have to take care of myself because there's nobody else who's going to do it.'

'I understand,' he replied, nodding. 'More than you can know.'

'If you want to fire me, I'll know why.'

'It sounds to me more like you're leaving.'

'I adore my job,' she said, her eyes filling with tears. 'I don't want to leave.'

'Then you may as well stay.' He leaned across her and opened her door, letting in a warm rush of rainy air. 'Since you're such a big girl, you don't need me to show you up to your apartment.'

She ran across the street, the rain beating into her face. She felt sick inside.

As she dried herself in her apartment, she found something hard in her pocket. It was the little jade monkey, clutching her prize but looking anxiously over her shoulder.

There was a hollow place in her heart. He hadn't even attempted to explain what had happened to Marcie. In a way, she was glad. She didn't want to hear any more lies.

And in any case, she knew exactly what had happened to Marcie. The talkative nurse in the sickbay had been delighted at the chance to gossip.

She adored Mr Zell. Absolutely mad about him. Worshipped the ground he trod on, if you know what I mean. She was a lovely, lovely girl, but then she started to look off-colour. Was even sick a couple of times in the office. Mr Zell ordered her to take a check-up. She wasn't pleased about that, I can tell you. But she couldn't refuse, could she? Next thing she's got the sack, and spirited off to some mysterious clinic in Zurich. I mean, anyone can put two and two together, can't they?

Oh, yes, it was easy to put two and two together. She knew exactly what kind of medical emergencies required instant dismissal and a mysterious visit to an expensive clinic. A clinic which specialised in little accidents. She knew all about that.

She was not going to suffer that pain again. Not even though she knew that she was never going to meet anyone like Anton Zell in her life again. She had once thought she was in love with Martin McCallum, but Anton was teaching her differently.

Because she, like Marcie, was also learning to adore Mr Zell. To be absolutely mad about him. To worship the ground he trod on.

She put the little jade monkey on her bedside table and curled up on the bed, not caring that her wet hair was dampening the pillow. Thunder rumbled across the bay from China.

Amy stared at the delicate green figure. How long was she going to be able to keep clutching her prize and looking over her shoulder?

Six weeks later, they flew back to Europe. The Zell Corporation was a partner in a big refinery project in Marseilles; one of the other companies, Barbusse Resources, had offered to buy out Anton's holdings. It would be a radical move, but it seemed to have found favour with Anton. They were going to hammer out the details of the deal.

They were also going to take advantage of being in the south of France in June to take a break on the Côte d'Azur and visit some of Anton's friends there, including Lady Carron, who had a villa at Cap d'Antibes. Amy was looking forward to seeing whether her surmise about the foot-long cigarette-holder was right.

Anton's private jet had seating for twelve passengers, but on this flight there were only the two of them in the luxurious cabin—Anton's financial team were already in Marseilles, at the negotiating table.

They had been in the air for three hours, having taken off in the warm dusk. It was now dark outside the cabin and they were both hungry. Amy went up to the galley and took the prepared meals—supplied by an aviation catering firm in Hong Kong—from the fridge to the microwave. As the first tray heated, she closed the curtains all down the Lear jet's body.

Anton was engrossed in papers relating to the shares deal that was coming up. She was amused as always to see that he was wearing glasses to read with. And as always when he was concentrating, he was so focused that he seemed barely aware of her presence as she walked past him. He did not even flinch when she opened the bottle of iced champagne with a loud pop. She had to fight down a mischievous urge to flip his glasses off his nose, just to get him to notice her.

For some reason, there was a large and beautiful parrot on board, sitting sleepily in a cage at the back of the cabin. It had something to do with the deal, Amy was not sure exactly what.

The microwave pinged. She took a meal up to the cockpit and gave it to the pilot, who was—disconcertingly—reading a book on trout fishing. Then she put her and Anton's meal in the microwave and took the champagne and two glasses to where Anton was sitting.

'Sorry to interrupt you,' she said, holding out the glass.

He tossed the papers aside. 'I've finished anyway,' he replied. 'What's for dinner?'

'I'm not sure, except that it looks a lot nicer than the usual airline food,' she said.

'And you look a lot nicer than the usual airline hostess,' he smiled.

She was delighted by the compliment. Since the disastrous visit to the jade market in Hong Kong, relations between them had been strained and restricted to work issues. Though she kept telling herself that was exactly what she most wanted, Amy ached for the intimacy that had once existed between them; an intimacy that seemed to have gone for ever.

She ached for his smiles, the way he used to tease her,

the way he used to touch her. But it was as though that had never been. And inside, she felt a terror that mounted every day—a terror that he would grow sick of having her around and would dismiss her and find someone more congenial.

The thought of *that* was unbearable.

'Well, thank you, sir; that has earned you a bottle of our complimentary champagne while you wait for the chef to add the final sauces.'

'Pour away, stewardess. I want to see beaded bubbles winking at the brim.'

'Coming right up, sir.'

Anton clinked his champagne glass against hers. 'God bless.'

'Bless you too,' she said, drinking.

'What are you smiling at?' he demanded.

'I always smile when I see you wearing glasses,' she said.

He took them off. 'I have grey hairs, too. You find the signs of age amusing?'

'You're not old,' she said soothingly, 'you're just in your prime.'

'So kind of you.'

'Think nothing of it.' She indicated his paperwork. 'Have you worked out your thoughts yet?'

'I worked them out long ago,' he said. 'I built the refinery about five years ago for a man named Henri Barbusse, of Barbusse Resources Incorporated. As part of the deal, I own forty per cent of the joint venture company, which is called Zell France. Henri is now a very rich man. He wants to buy out that forty per cent interest, which will make him sole owner of the facility.'

'Doesn't that mean you'll lose revenue?' she asked.

'Henri will offer a very good price,' Anton replied with a smile. 'The plant has a capacity of fifty thousand tons a year—and that's a lot of money. But I can use the cash elsewhere.'

'Such as where?'

'Well, the Marseilles facility is a finished mission. Right now, I'm excited by projects in some developing countries in south-east Asia—countries like Vietnam and Laos. I can use the money there, and they can use the technology. It's perfect for their economies.'

'How come?'

'Because it makes much more sense for them to recycle than to import. And in countries where the environment is especially fragile, reprocessing is a vital step.' He drank his champagne. 'These economies have been held back by politics and wars for decades. But I see them as the Asian tigers of the future. And I want a stake in their growth.'

'So you're not altogether St Anton,' she said drily.

'Not altogether,' he replied with a grin. 'But I do love those places, especially Vietnam. We'll be taking a trip there in a couple of months. You'll see just how beautiful it is.'

'Please tell me—what's the parrot for?'

'It's a macaw,' Anton replied. 'Henri Barbusse is mad about exotic birds. He has an aviary full of them. This is a gift for him. Getting the paperwork sorted out was a nightmare, I can tell you.'

Amy went to get the food. They settled down side by side in the ample seats to eat off the fold-down table. The trays actually contained a variety of beautifully prepared Chinese dishes in pretty little bowls. They both used chopsticks—living in Hong Kong, you soon got used to dispensing with knives and forks.

'This is a *very* superior airline. I've never had a whole plane to myself—not to mention the owner as my fellow passenger.'

'To me, space is the ultimate luxury,' he said. 'The main thing I remember from my childhood is never having any space of my own.'

'I know what you mean,' she said, sipping the icy champagne, which was delectable. 'When you're supernumerary, nothing is yours. You have to share everything. There's no place to call your own.'

'Except the space in your head,' he replied.

'Yes,' she said quietly. 'Except that. And they even try to take that away from you.'

Anton glanced at her. 'At the interview you told me that Jeffrey wasn't very happy to have an extra child to raise. Was he really that mean to you?'

Amy paused before answering. 'No, Jeffrey is a very good person. But he made sure I knew how lucky I was to be in his house. And my cousins took their cue from that. They made my life hell, especially when their father wasn't looking. And I could never complain to him—because I had to be so grateful.'

'And this is why you're such a hard case now?'

'Am I a hard case?' she said innocently.

'Tough as nails.' He selected a delicious sweet-and-sour prawn from his bowl and popped it into her mouth with deft chopsticks. While she chewed it appreciatively, he studied her. In the soft lighting of the cabin, his eyes were impenetrable. 'Tell me how they made your life hell.'

'Oh, I suppose I'm being melodramatic,' she said awkwardly. 'It wasn't that bad. But there were three of them—twin girls and a boy. The girls were much worse. They used to gang up on me and hurt me as much as they could. You know, girl things—pinching, pulling my hair, breaking my things.'

'Girls are expert torturers,' he said gently.

'Oh, yes. Sometimes they really hurt. They knew what they were doing. And I couldn't fight back, because the moment I did, they would tell Uncle Jeffrey and I would be punished even worse. They wanted to make me cry, but eventually I learned how to take it without crying. So as they got older, they started using words, instead.'

'What sort of words?'

'Predictable stuff. Why are you so interested?' she asked with an uneasy laugh.

'I'm interested in everything about you,' he said. 'Tell me what they used to say to you.'

Amy sighed. 'They used to tell me that my parents committed suicide because they knew I was the Devil's child.'

Anton's eyes widened. 'That's pretty good stuff. I had something similar in one place they sent me to. It gave me nightmares for years.'

'Me, too,' she said, half smiling at him. 'I used to dream the most awful things.'

'Gore and monsters. I know. What else did they say to you?'

'Oh, that nobody wanted me, everybody hated me. They told me I was ugly and wicked. That sort of thing. It got really bad when…'

'When?' he prompted as her voice trailed away.

There was a hot lump in her throat. 'I don't think I can tell you about it.'

Anton put his arm around her unexpectedly and drew her close to him. He drew her head gently onto his shoulder. 'Try,' he said in a quiet voice. 'It can only make it better to let it out.'

The warm smell of his skin was like a drug that intoxicated her senses, making it easier to say what was so hard. 'When I was twelve or thirteen and my body changed…'

'I understand.'

'They found out. They said such awful things. The girls were more or less my age but they hadn't started yet. I think they were jealous, in a way. I didn't dare tell anyone, not even Aunt Sheila. I didn't have a mother. I had to cope on my own. But every month after that was a nightmare, trying desperately to hide what was happening. But they always found out and then they would make life unbearable for me.'

He held her close, stroking her silky hair with a gentle hand. 'I'm sorry, Amy.'

'The twins started a year later and then it eased off. They were too busy concentrating on their own adolescence to worry about mine. And around then, they started just ignoring me. They'd done all the hurtful things they could think of. They got bored with the game and started leading their own lives. But I will always remember that as the worst year of my life.'

'But you got through it,' he said quietly. 'And now you know that if you could get through that, you can get through anything.'

She smiled against his shoulder. 'I supposed that's true.' It was heavenly to be cradled in his arms like this, to feel the warmth of his compassion, understanding but not sentimental, surrounding her. 'But I don't want to talk about me any more. I want to hear about you, Anton, about the foster homes you grew up in.'

'Changing the subject, I see.'

'Same subject, different viewpoint. You said some of your foster homes were very bad. Tell me about them.'

'The worst one? They wanted to make me as unhappy as they were. They beat me with a strap and locked me in a cupboard for days at a time.'

She felt suddenly sick. 'Oh, Anton, I'm so sorry. I didn't mean to touch such a painful memory.'

'I didn't mind the strap so much,' he said calmly. 'The cupboard was much worse. Because I wanted so desperately to go to school, you see. In the end, that saved me. The school sent someone round to the house to see why I was absent such a lot. So they took me out of there. I was kept in an orphanage for the next two years before they tried me with another foster family. The rest of my families were all wonderful. But somehow, after that, I always found myself on the outside, emotionally.'

'I'm so sorry,' she repeated. 'What happened to me was nothing like that.'

'It was probably just as bad,' he said. 'Inadequate and miserable people are the cruellest. They want to destroy everybody else's happiness. The worst part is not the insults or the bruises. It's not feeling loved.'

'Yes,' she whispered. 'I feel sick to my stomach, Anton. Poor little boy!'

He laughed. 'Don't tell me there's a weak spot in the armour plating!'

'I'm not armour plated as far as you're concerned,' she said softly. 'Always remember that, when you feel like teasing me.'

'I will. And please don't ever be afraid of telling me things,' he went on. 'I understand you better than you can know.'

'I believe you do,' she said, lifting her head to look at him. 'Thank you for listening—and for telling me about you.'

He kissed her mouth lightly. It was like a touch of velvet, but she drew away swiftly, as though she had been burned. 'Well, we're a couple of hard cases, aren't we?' he said, smiling at her with those amazing blue eyes.

Not trusting herself to reply after that kiss, Amy cleared away their trays and dumped everything in the service locker. Talking to him about her childhood, and catching a glimpse of his, had touched nerves deep inside her. She found that her hands were trembling with emotion. How strange to relive those memories here, high in the dark night, flying to France!

When she returned, Anton had produced blankets and pillows. 'Sleep beside me,' he commanded softly, 'in case nightmares come.'

'I won't have nightmares tonight,' she said.

'I'm not talking about you.' He reached up and turned off the overhead lights so that the cabin was in dimness.

The arm rest between the wide seats lifted up, and the backs went down, to produce a large and very welcoming bed. Amy kicked off her shoes and lay down beside him. His strong arms surrounded her, drawing her close. Though she was fully clothed in trousers and a blouse, and he in his customary jeans and silk shirt, the contact was as electric to her as though they were naked.

'We're the same, you and I,' he murmured, his warm breath brushing the sensitive skin of her throat. 'Always got our noses pressed to the window. Fogging up the glass and seeing things in a rosy, fuzzy glow.'

'I have no illusions, Anton.'

'You like to think you're so tough, Worthington,' he growled. 'Every day you get up and add another layer to that suit of armour you clank around in. I wonder if you can even see out of it any more.'

'It's safe in here,' she said. But lying in his arms she did not feel safe—not very safe at all.

CHAPTER SIX

AFTER the ceremonial presentation of the macaw—which Henri Barbusse seemed enchanted by—the negotiations began in a large, featureless hotel in Marseilles. It commanded panoramic views of the sea and had excellent conference facilities, but was otherwise about as exciting as a shoebox inside.

But the negotiations were fascinating. Sitting beside Anton and making sure he had all the papers he needed, Amy was in a perfect position to observe the subtle and not-so-subtle intricacies of the debate. In another time and place, Anton and Henri Barbusse might have been two generals commanding rival armies, and instead of millions of dollars, the profit and loss might have been in human blood.

As Anton had predicted, Henri Barbusse, a small, square-bearded man in his fifties, was offering a very large amount of money. His style was very different from Anton's; where Anton was relaxed and casual, Barbusse was a dandy, always impeccably starched and cufflinked; where Anton acted and spoke spontaneously, Barbusse was always smoothly produced, something of an actor. He reminded Amy of one of his own beloved birds, small, neat and always preening his feathers.

The main area of debate centred around exclusivity. While buying out the refinery, Barbusse wanted to prevent the Zell Corporation from building any similar plants for anyone else in France.

Anton smilingly conceded that the point was an important one. He seemed so relaxed about it that Amy began to be afraid he would give away too much. But watching how

69

Anton, with apparent casualness, worked the deal to his favour was an education in negotiation at the highest level.

By the second afternoon, Barbusse had conceded that Zell France would receive a royalty on every gallon for five more years, and Barbusse Resources Inc. had to order at least one more refinery within two years, and discuss the possibility of a third and possibly more plants. The additional refineries were to be installed at locations already belonging to Zell France or its partners, and Barbusse was to compensate Zell accordingly.

The papers were ready to sign and a Press conference was called to showcase the agreement. Media interest was high, and TV cameras as well as a bevy of newspaper reporters were on hand to film the signing and tape statements from both Anton and Barbusse.

To celebrate the conclusion of the deal, the next night Henri Barbusse took the whole negotiating team out to a magnificent dinner which began with Marseilles's most famous dish, *bouillabaisse*, which—as Anton took great pleasure in telling her—was made from the deadly stonefish, proceeded through lobster thermidor, and concluded with an assortment of liqueurs and nougat.

. Amy was wearing a stretch dress in dark blue which flattered her figure, and she could tell she was getting a lot of male attention, which pleased her ego. Among the male eyes which dwelled on her curves were Anton's. He had not seen her in going-out clothes, she realised; in Hong Kong she dressed very formally, for the office; and when they were in the field, she wore loose casuals in khakis and browns. By the expression in his eyes, he was enjoying the glimpse of her curves which the blue dress afforded!

After dinner they were taken to a cabaret, which was funny and sophisticated, and then on to a club. It was a delightful evening and she was very taken aback when Henri Barbusse asked her to dance in between numbers.

On the crowded dance-floor, Barbusse was unexpectedly flirtatious. 'Where did my friend Anton find such an angel as you?' he demanded.

'I assure you, he doesn't consider me an angel, Monsieur Barbusse!'

'You are divine, my dear. A symphony in blue and gold! I have been watching you for these past two days. If conditions with Zell are ever less than heavenly, you come straight to me, OK? I will make all your dreams come true!'

'I'll bear that in mind,' she said tactfully.

'You do that.'

Barbusse had gyrated her into a corner of the dance-floor from which there was no escape and now he closed in. Amy found herself enfolded in octopus arms, with an insistent pelvis bumping hers suggestively.

'You do that, little bird,' he said hoarsely into her ear. 'Bear me in mind!'

'I will, I promise.'

Wishing she knew some jiu-jitsu, she tried to evade the amorous millionaire. A scented beard brushed her cheek. 'Do not fly away, my little bird,' he murmured. 'Tell me what Zell pays you. I will double it.'

'I'm happy with my salary!'

'I will make you happier.'

'But I like living in Hong Kong,' she replied, trying to squirm out of the embrace.

A hand closed around her breast. 'You will grow tired of it—come and live in Paris!'

'I'll think about it,' she repeated, jerking the hand away from her breast.

'Take my card, little pigeon,' he murmured, 'you have the most beautiful bosom I ever saw.' He produced a gilt-edged card with his number on it and tried to slip it into her cleavage. She intercepted it as gracefully as she could. She managed to evade both the scented beard and the exploring pelvis at last, and when the number ended scampered back to Anton with relief.

Anton was smiling lazily at her. 'What was that interesting dance you were doing with *cher* Henri?'

'It's called *Dodge the Oil Magnate*,' she said breathlessly, adjusting her dress.

'Or maybe, *Dances with Wolves*?'

'Right. Or *In a Tight Corner with a Tycoon*.'

'And what was he whispering in your shell-like ear?'

'He was offering me a job at twice what you pay me.'

'No, really? It looked like he was demonstrating some of the perks of the job, too.'

'You are a pig,' she said, and he laughed out loud.

'Weren't you tempted by the generous offer?'

'Of course I was tempted. He gave me his card.'

'Yes, I saw him post something down your front. Such a delicious letter box. But I'm surprised Henri's little offering didn't get lost in the recesses of your costume.'

'I'm beginning to wish I'd worn something less *décolleté*,' she said ruefully.

'If you've got them, flaunt them. Especially if they're doubling your salary every time you trot them out.'

'They're not that big, for heaven's sake.'

'Pushing them in Henri's face probably made them look larger,' he said, deadpan.

'I was *not* pushing them in his face!'

'Yes, you were. You can push them in my face now, Worthington. Unless you're too out of breath?'

He took her hand, and, breathless as she was, she went back on the floor with him to dance.

Dancing with Anton was much nicer than dancing with Henri Barbusse. He was graceful and light on his feet and made no attempt to paw her. When the music changed to a slow, dreamy number, he took her gently in his arms and held her lightly but firmly against his strong body. He danced so well that she could almost forget that she had feet at all, and just drift along to his rhythm.

'So?' he asked her. 'Has Marseilles been interesting?'

'I've learned more in the last couple of days than in the past five years,' she said.

'What have you learned?'

'For one thing, that Anton Zell can have it all.'

'What do you mean?'

'Well, you came here to sell your share in a refinery. But it's ended up that you're still going to share in the profits for five more years, build up to two new refineries, and sell some very expensive industrial real estate. You're a very clever man.'

He brushed her cheek with his. 'Flattery will get you nowhere.'

'I'm not flattering you, Mr Fox. Merely commenting on your cunning.'

'Can I comment on your beauty?'

'Flattery will get you nowhere. But go ahead if you must.'

'You are by far the most beautiful woman here,' he said, his breath warm against her neck. 'But that's the least of it. You're probably also the most beautiful woman in France tonight.'

'Only probably?'

'There *are* twenty-five million others. One has to be cautious in business estimates.'

'Oh, so this is a business conversation we're having?' she said, feeling his powerful stomach muscles brushing against hers.

'A wage negotiation.'

'Am I in line for a raise?'

'Well, I don't want you going over to the opposition. I like you just where you are.'

'I don't plan on going over to Henri Barbusse any time soon.'

'But you have kept his card.'

'A girl has to have a back-up plan.'

'I see. So what do you want, Worthington? More money—or more perks?'

Her breasts pressed against his chest as they moved together. 'Tell me about the perks.'

'I tried to give you a jade bracelet, but you turned me down flat.'

'Ah, yes,' she said wryly. 'Don't think I didn't get the symbolism of that particular perk.'

'Symbolism?'

'Oh yes.' Her hair brushed his cheek. 'You wanted to put a bangle carved with a dragon around my wrist.'

'Correct.'

'Giving everybody the message that I belonged to the big dragon himself.'

'Or maybe that the big dragon belonged to you.'

'Hah! That'll be the day!'

His mouth touched her temple, then her cheek, then the corner of her mouth. 'But I was trying to tell you how beautiful you are,' he murmured. 'That dress suits you perfectly. Are you wearing any underwear beneath it?'

'Of course.'

'It doesn't show.'

'It's very expensive underwear.'

'So I'm clearly already paying you too much.'

She lifted her face to his to retort, but he didn't give her a chance. His lips sealed hers with a firm, possessive kiss that made her bones melt. 'Mr Fox,' she whispered, looking up at him with shining eyes, 'you are taking liberties!'

'I am sorry,' he said, not sounding apologetic in the slightest, 'talking about your underwear—or the absence of it—made me lose my head for a second.'

'"I lost my head" is a very feeble excuse.'

'Better than, "I lost my underwear".'

She burst out laughing. Luckily the slow number ended, and the pace picked up, and she was able to beg him to let her go back to the table for a drink.

The party was still going strong in the early hours of the morning, when Amy started to droop and begged for permission to go back to the hotel to bed.

'I'll take you,' Anton said.

'Oh, please don't leave the party,' she replied, 'I'll go back to the hotel on my own, there's no need for you to escort me!'

'I've had enough too, honey bunny. And I think Henri wants an excuse to get back to his exotic birds, *n'est-ce pas, Henri*?'

'It is rather late,' Barbusse said with a smile, 'and you had better get your own bird of paradise back to her nest before she puts her beautiful head under her wing and goes to sleep!' He kissed Amy's hand lingeringly. 'I will see you tomorrow, Anton.'

Five minutes later, after shaking a dozen hands and accepting fulsome congratulations, she and Anton were walking out of the club.

It was a beautiful, clear night. Their hotel was a ten-minute walk away, so they elected to stroll back along the Promenade.

'When Monsieur Barbusse wakes up tomorrow morning and reads that contract, he may have rather more than a hangover!' she commented as they walked.

Anton burst out laughing. He put her arm around her waist and drew her close, so that they were walking in unison. 'Believe me, Henri is a better businessman than you give him credit for. He's going to make a lot of money out of this deal. And I have the capital I need to expand in south-east Asia. Nobody got robbed here.'

'Just remind me never to play poker with you,' she said.

'Look! The moon in June.'

A full moon was hanging over the sea, making a river of silver light along the waves. They stopped to admire it. She rested her head on Anton's shoulder dreamily.

'Here you are, orphan boy,' she said. 'Now an industrial giant, with interests all over the world. What's it like to come from having so little to having all this?'

He stroked her hair. 'There's an old saying—a man only has what he can hold in his two hands. Looked at from that point of view, I have always had what you call ''all this''. And I will always have nothing.'

'You own yourself,' she replied quietly, 'and that's more than most men have.'

'Or most women. And you own yourself, Amy.'

'It doesn't always feel like that,' she said in a small voice.

'You're the most self-possessed woman I know,' he said, smiling. 'The problem is trying to get you to let go now and then.'

'For example?'

'For example, you know that I am mad about you, but you won't let me near you.'

She shivered at his caress. 'You're near me now.'

'True, in a brotherly sort of way. But—for example, if I tried to kiss you now, you would jump like a scalded cat.'

Amy closed her eyes. She was not so sure of that. 'Cats are animals that like things on their own terms,' she said.

'Something that every cat-lover knows,' he said, his voice purring. 'Now, you see, Henri Barbusse is a bird-lover. He likes to put them in cages and admire them in captivity. I prefer you spitting and scratching.'

'I would never leave you to go to Henri Barbusse, even if he tripled my salary.'

'So you are a little bit mad about me, too?' he asked softly, kissing her ear.

Shudders ran down her spine. 'No,' she whispered, 'I just like my job, Mr Zell.'

'That's all?'

'That's all! Now take your wildcat home before she starts scratching and spitting!'

The yellow moon followed them as they walked back to the hotel, holding hands.

With everything concluded in Marseilles, they were free to go to the Côte d'Azur for a short break. They were to be house guests at the Antibes villa of Lady Carron—whom Anton had described as a troublesome shareholder, but who, Amy suspected by her imperious phone calls, might be something more.

Anton rented an open-topped Mercedes sports car—which he claimed was *de rigueur* in the south of France in summer—and they drove in a leisurely way from Marseilles along the coast. She was getting on so well with him lately that everything was like a happy dream.

They drove through a sunlit Mediterranean landscape of vineyards, pine forests and wide beaches, stopping along the way to have lunch in the garden of a country restaurant called La Sirène, where the food and the wine were magnificent.

'So the people we're going to be staying with in Antibes are major shareholders in the Zell Corporation?' she asked Anton over the gooey and delicious *tarte Tatin*.

'It's a complicated story,' he replied. 'To try and simplify it: Sir Robert Carron was a financier who backed me when I started up. The first few refineries I built were financed with loans from him. His firm also steered us through the rights issue when we went public a few years later. He had confidence in us so he bought several blocks of shares. He married Lavinia quite recently. She was much younger than Robert. When he died, she inherited a lot of his shareholdings—so she now has a twenty per cent stake in the Zell Corporation.'

'That gives her quite a voice.'

'Exactly. Hence this visit. Lavinia is young, but very shrewd—and very strong-willed. She has her own idea about the direction the corporation should be taking. So I've got two choices. Buy her out—or keep her sweet.'

'And keeping her sweet is cheaper,' Amy said, her voice a lot more acid than the mouthful of buttery, caramelised apple she had just swallowed.

'Cheaper *and* more fun,' he said with a wicked glint in his eyes.

'I see,' Amy said, even more sourly. 'The dear departed Sir Robert had good taste, did he?'

'She's not particularly beautiful. But she is interesting. As you will see.'

'I can hardly wait.'

'It will be an education,' he promised.

'It's so peaceful here,' Amy sighed, looking up at the cypresses and gnarled olive trees all around, not wanting to leave. It was hot and the chirring of cicadas was soporific. 'I think this must be an enchanted garden. I'm very glad to be out of Marseilles.'

'So am I,' Anton replied. 'At least it's stopped you putting the moves on poor Henri.'

'I was *not* putting the moves on him,' she said indignantly.

'Yes, you were. It was scandalous. You were as bad as *her*.' He pointed to the old stone fountain, in the shape of a seductive and very bosomy mermaid, after which the restaurant was obviously named.

'I was not,' she retorted. 'Henri is a randy old goat, and you know it.'

'He did appear to be ripping your bodice.'

'He was trying to give me his card.'

'Is that what you mermaids call it?'

She glanced at the statue of the mermaid. 'Anyway, I don't have her attributes.'

'Just as well,' Anton said silkily. 'I'm very glad that you're woman from the navel down, and not halibut.'

She giggled. 'You are wayward, dear master. And you don't know much about mermaids.'

'Enlighten me,' he invited, filling her glass.

'Well,' she said, 'mermaids do occasionally mate with mortal men. They lose their fish tails and look just like ordinary women. But it's usually only for a year or two. They pine for the sea. And one stormy night, they change back again without warning. They disappear. Go back to the sea.'

'Leaving a heartbroken mortal man?' he suggested.

'And the bed full of fish scales.'

'So you could be a mermaid after all?' he asked, looking into her eyes

Amy batted her eyelids. 'You never know.'

'Hmm. That might explain some of your peculiar ways.'

'It might, indeed,' she agreed.

'And tell me,' he went on softly, 'what induces a mermaid to mate with a mortal man?'

'When they fall in love.' She rested her chin on her hand, smiling at him. 'But it hardly ever happens.'

'And when they do fall in love, isn't there any way of keeping them from turning back into mermaids?'

'Only one way.'

'Tell me.'

'They have to have a baby. A mortal child. Then they forget the sound of the crashing waves and become human women for ever.'

'So if I want to keep you, I have to make you pregnant?'

She had been lost in the romantic warmth of their bantering, but those words brought a sudden chill into her soul. 'That wouldn't be very wise,' she said, looking away.

'I'm only teasing,' he said gently. 'I just want to know how to get a mermaid to fall in love with me.'

'I told you, it hardly ever happens.'

'Like hurricanes in Hertford, Hereford and Hampshire?'

'That's right, Professor Higgins.'

Anton smiled faintly at her tense expression. 'And the maiden turned back into a cold stone statue. What did I say?'

'Nothing,' she said.

He sighed. 'Well, if we're going to reach Antibes by suppertime, I suppose we'd better get moving.'

Amy felt her heart ache as they left the enchanted garden with the stone mermaid. Why was it that in the most heavenly moments, something always popped up, like an ugly jack-in-the-box, to bring her back down to earth?

CHAPTER SEVEN

LAVINIA CARRON'S villa was not in Antibes itself, but situated in the rocky, sun-baked hills behind the town. It was a very commanding position, with spreading views of the harbour and the old town, with Nice visible in the distance, on the other side of the bay.

The house itself was very large, made of stone, and obviously two or three centuries old. No expense had been spared in its restoration. As they drove along the immaculately gravelled driveway, Amy glimpsed modern sculptures among the surgically pruned flowering shrubs and tall cypresses of the gardens. There was a spectacular rose garden, too, the flowers arranged into geometric beds according to colour and height.

They pulled up in a courtyard with a gleaming and rather magnificent marble fountain featuring three life-sized lions spouting water from snarling muzzles.

'Eighteenth-century Italian,' Anton told her. 'Imported from Florence by Lavinia. It was rather too mossy for her taste, so she had it sand-blasted.'

'How hygienic,' Amy commented.

As they were getting out of the car, they heard the clop of a horse's hooves. A woman on a big bay gelding came trotting into the courtyard. She jumped off lightly.

'Anton! Darling! How lovely to see you.'

Lady Carron was a slim woman with brown hair and a lean, suntanned face, in which large, violet eyes glowed brightly. As Anton had said, her features were interesting rather than conventionally beautiful, with an aquiline nose and a rather thin mouth; but she was certainly a very attractive woman nonetheless. And she looked very good in her boots, jodhpurs and white cotton shirt.

She kissed Anton warmly on each cheek. 'You look wonderful, darling boy. Quite untarnished by Eastern suns.'

'You look like a bowl of choice fruit yourself, Lavinia,' he grinned. 'This is my assistant, Amy Worthington. Amy, Lavinia Carron.'

'Pleased to meet you, Lady Carron,' Amy said, resisting the urge to curtsey like some pre-Revolutionary French peasant.

'Call me Lavinia, please.' She gave Amy a hand which was small, strong, and still encased in a pale cream leather riding glove. 'So you're the new girl! I hope you've been looking after this naughty boy of mine?'

'I have been trying,' Amy said lightly.

'Well, you can have a rest, you poor child. I'll take over from now on.' The glitter in the lavender eyes made sure Amy understood it was an order. Seen from close up, Lavinia Carron was not quite as young as the trim figure would suggest, but she was obviously very fit. She pulled off the gloves and took Anton's arm in a firm brown hand. 'Come and have a drink on the terrace, you naughty boy; you must be parched in this frightful heat.'

The invitation did not include Amy, obviously. Anton threw her a rueful glance over his shoulder as Lavinia marched him off, leaving Amy with the servants who had emerged to take the bags and lead the horse away. She gave him a death's-head grin in reply.

The house had been furnished in the kind of taste that took a large budget and a very competent interior designer. It was also spotlessly neat and clean. Anton had been allocated a large room overlooking the garden and the blue Mediterranean in the distance. Her own room was very much smaller and darker, and boasted a view of the stables—where a large pile of manure was being forked into a cart by a young groom, no doubt destined for Lady Carron's roses.

She unpacked, trying not to feel resentful at having been so instantly and efficiently separated from Anton. Though he treated her as a friend and equal, there was no reason to expect that his wealthy friends would behave the same way.

Feeling very much the poor relation, she tried to repair her appearance—her hair had been dishevelled in the open-topped car—with a quick shower and a change of clothing. She had just finished dressing in trousers and a deep pink shirt when Anton knocked at her door and let himself in.

'Come and have a drink,' he said. 'You must meet the other guests.'

'Are you sure I'm wanted?' she asked. 'I could just go down the back stairs to the pantry and get a bowl of gruel.'

He laughed, deep blue eyes dancing. 'You'll get used to Lavinia. She has a certain style.'

'So I see.'

'Nice view,' Anton commented, deadpan, looking out of her window.

She joined him. Lady Carron's glossy bay gelding was now being assiduously brushed in front of his stable door by the same young groom. 'I don't believe that horse has been ridden at all,' she said grimly. 'In this heat, both she and it would have been covered in sweat and dust in ten minutes.'

'Perhaps she was just setting off when we arrived.'

'Or perhaps she wanted you to see how trim she looked in her Lara Croft outfit. Please tell me she isn't entertaining her guests in bespoke riding boots from W&H Gidden, with silver spurs a-jingling?'

'She is not wearing spurs, as you very well know.'

'Now, you see, a *real* lady would never wear jodhpurs to greet her guests. She just wants you to look at her backside.'

'Well, being mistress of the house means you get to choose what view each guest gets,' he said, evidently amused by her ill-temper.

'Which is how you and I both wound up looking at the rear end of a horse,' she said sweetly, studying herself in the mirror. 'I'm ready to go down now, Master Anton.'

The party assembled on the terrace was not very large. In addition to herself and Anton, there were two other couples, one Swiss, one French, and a solitary Englishman named Mike, who attached himself in a rather melancholy way to Amy. The one factor they all had in common was the unmistakable trappings of serious wealth—costly jewellery, watches, teeth and facelifts gleamed in the light of the setting sun.

An unobtrusive maid served the drinks. Lavinia effortlessly steered Anton over to the other end of the terrace, where loud explosions of laughter were punctuating a funny story being told by the Swiss woman, who was a spectacular blonde with a lot of bosom on show. Her husband, a banker, was egging her on.

The Englishman, Mike, who turned out to be Lavinia's neighbour, had evidently already consumed several of the bright-orange drinks which he favoured.

'I live in the next villa along,' he told Amy. 'Can't see my house from here. Lavinia owns practically the whole hillside.'

'It's such a wonderful setting,' Amy said sincerely. 'You're very lucky. Do you live here all the year round?'

'I do. Lavinia doesn't. She also has a house in London and a place in Barbados.'

'Wow.'

'My house isn't quite as swish as Lavinia's,' Mike said,

eyeing the flawless regularity of the stonework with an alcohol-bleared eye. 'See how smooth the masonry is? When she was doing up the place, she had the stonemason go over the whole house with a fine-tooth comb. Every stone that was a funny shape or colour was ripped out and replaced.'

'She likes all her ducks in a row.'

'Oh, yes. A bit of class, Lavinia is. Asset to the community. You should see her, flying in with the chopper. She got her helicopter licence last year. Orange jumpsuit and mirror shades. Delicious sight.'

'Even better than in jodhpurs and riding boots?' Amy asked sympathetically.

'Just about as good,' Mike said sadly. 'Been trying to get her to marry me ever since old Bob died. Don't suppose I've got much hope.'

'Keep trying,' Amy advised. 'You know the old saying? Nothing propinks like propinquity.'

'Eh?'

'Being a neighbour,' she explained gently. 'You're in a good position.'

'Right,' Mike said, tapping his inflamed nose wisely. 'That's just earned you another drink.'

The sun went down, giving way to a velvety and cicada-inspired night. Dinner was served in the dining-room, which was an impressive chamber furnished with curvaceous mahogany Chippendale and what appeared to be real Impressionist paintings in heavy frames on the walls.

As on the terrace, Amy had been paired with Mike, who by now was even sadder and more inebriated. But the party was small enough that she could hear all the conversations that were going on.

Lavinia had finally changed out of her tailored riding gear and was wearing a violet sheath dress which intensified her eyes and showed off her slim, suntanned arms and shoulders—as well as two apple-like breasts that might or might not have owed their firmness to a judicious addition of silicone.

'You look wonderful, Lavinia,' Anton said appreciatively, 'like something from a Paul Jacoulet print.'

'Thank you, sweet boy,' she purred in reply. Amy spread her napkin studiously in her lap, hoping she wasn't going to throw up.

The meal started with *moules à la marinière*, succulent mussels cooked in sherry. The main course was a huge baked fish in a rich Provençal sauce. Lavinia was watching with a hawk eye as the maid served each guest in turn.

'Now tell me, you wicked boy,' she said to Anton, smiling at him lazily over her Baccarat wine glass, 'what is all this nonsense about turning the Zell Corporation into some kind of ecological charitable trust?'

'I've never thought of myself as a charity,' he replied with a smile. 'But you know as well as I do that the petrochemical industry doesn't exactly have a shining record on environmental issues.'

'And pray, who cares about *that* apart from a few lunatic fringe groups?'

'Well, we all ought to care about it,' Anton replied, 'since we all have to live in the same world, breathe the same air and drink the same water.'

'Drink the stuff that comes out of the tap?' Lavinia said disapprovingly. 'You bad boy, you know I only touch Vichy or Perrier.'

Anton smiled. 'Well, I hope you don't plan to start buying your own air, too. You wouldn't be nearly so pretty wearing a scuba mask.'

'You're just trying to annoy me,' Lavinia said in a purring voice. She reached out a slender brown hand and began to stroke his arm. It was a gesture of unmistakable possession.

'These projects of yours to refine used oil aren't nearly as profitable as big, old-fashioned refineries.'

'I haven't noticed that profits have dropped lately,' he replied mildly.

'Not yet—but they will do if you let the opposition take over your traditional business while you gallop off on your new hobby-horse.' The slim, tanned fingers curled on his forearm, and the pearly nails dug in hungrily, assessing the springy muscles. 'And *recycling*—that must be the least stylish word in the English language, for heaven's sake!'

Anton laughed. 'It ought to be the most stylish word in the English language.'

'And anyway, what's the percentage in cleaning up old oil that's already been used?'

'The percentage is that we're teaching people to re-utilise a finite resource. When the planet's oil supplies run out, we're going to have to start cleaning up the old oil anyway. But we won't be able to do that if it's all been dumped in holes in the ground!'

'Oh, Anton! Who's interested in all that Doomsday talk?'

'People who care about the environment, for one thing. For another, people who want to offset expensive oil imports.'

Lavinia lowered her eyelids over amethyst eyes. 'But dear boy, don't we *want* the price of oil to go up?'

'Not unless you're happy to see the world caught up in another oil crisis, with all that that entails.'

Heinz, the banker, leaned forward. 'It doesn't do to turn your business into an aid organisation, old boy. You've sold off the Marseilles refinery, which was making a fortune.'

'The deal looks pretty good to me,' Anton replied easily.

'Maybe the stockholders will feel less certain. And launching new technology is a risky business, whatever fine moral principles you espouse. As Lavinia's banker, I have to agree with her. Remember your shareholders. Don't get carried away by a dream.'

'My whole business is built on a dream,' Anton said. 'The day I stop dreaming will be the day I stop living. My latest dream is of a cleaner world where our oil supplies last for centuries longer. But I've made it clear at the last few shareholders' meetings that refining raw stock is an increasingly crowded field. We have to look to new technologies if we're to keep growing. Refining used oil is the way of the future. And as crude oil gets scarcer and more expensive, it can only become more important. To everybody, not just developing nations. It's a new field, yes, but we're going to be dominant in it.'

'Darling boy,' Lavinia drawled, 'I like to see lots and lots of money in my bank account. Nothing else matters to me. I don't care if that means chimneys belching smoke or the occasional oil-spill on some remote coastline—as long as it isn't ours.'

'Hear, hear,' Mike said in a slurred voice.

'We're in the oil business,' Lavinia went on. She was still kneading Anton's arm insistently. 'If the price of Mr Jones filling his gas tank goes up, that just means more profits for you and me!'

'But it *is* on your coastline,' Amy heard herself say.

Lavinia turned cold eyes on her. 'I beg your pardon?'

'It is on your coastline,' Amy repeated. 'That sea that you gaze at may look blue, but it's more polluted than anywhere else in the Mediterranean.'

'That's an exaggeration, to put it kindly,' Lavinia said grimly. 'Everything you have eaten tonight comes out of that sea.'

'Yes, and I'm afraid that this delicious fish we're eating is full of heavy metals like mercury, cadmium and lead. And those tasty *moules à la marinière* contain some very colourful toxins, including polynuclear aromatic hydrocarbons. It all comes from the oil refineries at Marseilles. Nobody's doing very much about it, except people like Anton. So it *is* on your coastline, you see.'

Lavinia's mouth and eyes showed her anger. 'We have all heard these scare stories for years. But nobody has actually died yet.'

'Millions of fish and shellfish have died,' Amy retorted. 'Every year, countless tons of used oil just get dumped into the environment,' she went on. 'With Anton's technology, all of that could be turned back into a valuable resource and reused. And his shareholders have no cause to complain. Profits are well up for the tenth quarter in a row. I think you should just let him do what he does best, sit back, and enjoy the profits.'

'Amy,' Anton said in a low, but warning voice.

'I'm sorry, perhaps that was unpardonably rude,' Amy said, flushing hotly. 'It's a subject I feel strongly about.'

Lavinia's hand was clamped hard on Anton's arm now, as though she had suddenly become aware of a dangerous challenge to her authority. In her violet sheath, she resembled some exotic snake about to strike. 'Well, dear Snow White,' she said thinly, 'having eaten my poisoned apple, when can we expect you to fall into a deep—and silent—slumber?'

'Amy is certainly right about the bottom line,' Anton said, stepping swiftly into the breach as Amy coloured even more hotly. 'The new technology and its spin-offs look set to earn us even bigger profits. I'm going to announce expansion plans at the next board meeting.'

His calm voice seemed to soothe Lavinia's ire as he explained the network of refineries he was planning to build over the next years, but Amy felt as though a jagged stone had lodged in her throat. She hadn't meant to get so carried away, and insult Lavinia Carron at her own table. Or to embarrass Anton by being so obstreperous that her hostess had told her to shut up. He was probably furious with her and she would be lucky to keep her job. Most likely, she would be finding herself unemployed by tomorrow morning.

Truth to tell, perhaps it had been watching those sharp, pearly nails raking Anton's skin that had enraged her so much, not just the conversation.

Whatever her excuse, she was now plainly about as welcome at the dinner party as a pile of horse manure. The best thing she could do was cart herself off as soon as possible and spread herself on the rose beds.

Accordingly, as soon as they adjourned from the table and moved to the salon, Amy offered a quiet apology about feeling tired and excused herself. Lavinia ignored her utterly. Anton, cornered between the hostess and her Swiss banker, was too busy to do more than glance at her as she left. Slinking up to bed, Amy felt tears of mortification pricking behind her eyelids. She was hurried on her way by a comment from Lavinia which—luckily—she did not hear, but which brought a guffaw of laughter from the other guests.

She lay in her lonely bed in a state of misery. Despite the huge size of the house, she could occasionally catch bursts of laughter or music from downstairs. It gave her the sensation of being a child again, exiled to her room for some fresh piece of bad behaviour, eavesdropping on a life which she was not permitted to share.

She was still far from sleep when, hours later, her door swung open and the light flared on.

Dazzled, her eyes hurting, she sat up in bed. A tall figure was towering over her.

'Anton?'

'What the hell were you playing at tonight?' he demanded savagely. 'Have you lost your mind?'

'Anton, I'm so sorry,' she said abjectly. 'I don't know what got into me.'

'Didn't you listen to *anything* I told you on the way up here?'

'Yes, I promise that I did listen—'

'Lavinia holds a twenty per cent stake in the corporation. Can you understand that?'

'Yes,' she whispered.

'And she doesn't like the new direction we're taking. The idea was to reassure her—not antagonise her. *And* her bank manager, for heaven's sake.' Her eyes were growing used to the light, but it did not give her any consolation to see that his mouth was a harsh line and that his eyes were almost black with anger. 'What the hell did you think you were playing at?'

His tone was so angry that she was on the verge of tears. 'I didn't mean to mess things up for you, Anton. When she started talking so callously, I just lost it. Are you going to fire me?'

'Lavinia has specifically requested exactly that,' he replied.

Her eyes welled. 'Oh.'

The sight of her wet eyes seemed to make him pause. 'Don't do that,' he snapped.

'Sorry.' She blotted her tears. 'I've been lying here counting the ways in which I made a fool of myself tonight.'

He sat on the bed beside her. 'It was certainly a spectacular display of foolishness.'

She cringed at the comment. 'I'm so sorry,' she said with a lump in her throat. 'Am I fired?'

He paused before replying. Her heart fluttered like a broken bird. 'If I don't fire you,' he said in a calmer voice, 'Lavinia will be even angrier.'

'Then you'd better fire me,' she whispered.

'I don't take orders from anyone,' he said shortly. 'And I have never fired anyone for speaking their mind. Besides, you said nothing but the truth. I'm going to risk Lavinia's wrath.' His eyes narrowed terrifyingly. 'But if you say or do one thing more to annoy her while we're here, I will personally throttle you.'

'I'll be as silent as a stone,' she said fervently. 'I'm really sorry, Anton. I don't know what got into me.'

'The point of this visit is so I can make sure she doesn't create a fuss at the next board meeting and panic other shareholders. Do you think you can manage to stay in the background for a few days?'

'I'll go for long, solitary walks,' she vowed. 'You can let her squeeze your arm and tell her she looks like a portrait by Paul Jacoulet as much as you like.'

'Good,' he said.

'Who is Paul Jacoulet, by the way?'

'A French artist who made drawings of beautiful women.'

'Oh. How cultured you are. Those breasts aren't real, you know.'

'Amy,' he said warningly.

She cursed herself. This was becoming a kind of insanity. 'Sorry. I will behave, I promise.'

She felt his hand stroke her hair. 'I know it's going to be hard for you,' he said softly. 'You looked like an angel tonight—try and be one for a while.'

She turned her face so that her soft cheek rested in the palm of his hand. 'How far do you intend to go along the path of charm?'

'Trust me.' He drew her close and kissed her cheek. 'It's all in a good cause.'

'I do trust you.' It required only a small tilt of her head—or did he tilt his?—for her lips to brush his.

'My sweet Amy,' he whispered. He kissed her lips again, then a third time. His mouth was so sweet, so tender. She felt herself melting. She slipped her arms around his neck, the ache in her heart turning into a surging warmth.

His tongue searched for hers, found it, caressed it longingly. A thrill of desire ran through her. She was finally learning to trust him. When he kissed her like this, doubts fled like shadows from the rising sun.

Anton's warm hand touched her breasts. She was wearing only a light summer negligée. Her nipples tightened with delight at his touch, pressing into his palm as he cupped her curves. At least *they* were real, she thought, exulting in his touch.

'I want you so much, Amy!' he whispered.

But at that moment, an unmistakable voice floated along the corridor. 'Anton? Have you got lost, darling boy? Where are you?'

'Damn her,' Anton said, with a catch in his voice. He kissed her eyelids. 'She wants us all to go into Antibes to see the moonlight on the sea or some such nonsense.'

'I was about to throw you out, anyway,' Amy said with an effort. She pushed him away with the last of her strength. 'Duty calls. Go where glory awaits you.'

Anton laughed softly. 'Aye aye. Sweet dreams, angel girl.'

He slipped out of her room. Shortly afterwards, Amy thought she heard Lavinia Carron's fluting laugh.

She curled into a ball, feeling his kiss still burning her lips, her nipples still aching at his touch. What she would give to be with Anton for the rest of this night, looking at the moonlight on the sea.

Or some such nonsense.

She had to get a grip on herself. Jealousy was the green-eyed monster that mocked what it fed upon. She would never have dreamed of letting Anton get so close to her—except that it hurt so much to see him being appropriated by Lavinia Carron!

What a mystery the female heart was! She should have been delighted to have the pressure taken off her. Having rejected Anton's advances countless times, in countless subtle and not-so-subtle ways, having convinced herself that he was a heartless rake, what was bringing these tears to her eyes?

CHAPTER EIGHT

SHE would always look back on the rest of that week as one of the most miserable periods of her life.

To begin with, the next morning, Gerda Meyer, the Swiss woman, came down with a violent stomach upset. In light of Amy's unfortunate remarks the evening before about toxins in seafood, it was hardly an auspicious event. Each time Lavinia looked Amy's way there seemed to be an almost perceptible rumble of psychic thunder.

By way of atonement—for the crime, presumably, of not having been summarily fired for insolence—Amy found herself cast in the role of nurse and comforter to Gerda, who was not in any way an easy patient. Her husband, Heinz, seemed to be eager to stay as far away from the bed of suffering as possible.

Bringing Gerda her umpteenth tisane of the day, Amy found the sufferer well enough to be sitting up accusingly, her blonde hair in disarray.

'Why did you have to talk about such horrible things last night?' she wailed. 'You have upset me terribly! What if I have been poisoned?'

'I'm sure it's just a simple tummy bug,' Amy said soothingly. 'It happens in the summertime, especially after eating shellfish.'

'Do not mention shellfish!' Gerda clutched at the tisane and gulped it down. 'Oh, my poor stomach! And I look such a fright,' she moaned, peering into her hand-mirror. 'The least you can do is help me look presentable so I can receive visitors.'

'Of course,' Amy sighed. She fetched Gerda's brush—

silver-backed and monogrammed—and started brushing the heavy blonde tresses into order.

'Where are Lavinia and Anton?' Gerda demanded.

Gritting her teeth at the way the two names had been lumped together as a self-evident pair, Amy replied, 'They've gone for a ride together on the horses.'

Indeed, she had seen them walking off along the hillside together just after lunch, looking very companionable. It was as though she and Anton inhabited different planets today. He had barely spoken to her. His attention had been focused on Lavinia.

'They will be married soon,' Gerda said. 'Please be careful! You are pulling my hair out by the roots!'

'Sorry,' Amy said thickly. 'What makes you say they're going to get married?'

Gerda giggled. 'Oh, Lavinia has made up her mind. And what Lavinia wants, Lavinia gets!'

'You mean Anton Zell has no say in the matter?'

'What would he want to say?'

'He might want to protest.'

'Protest?' Gerda asked in perplexity. 'They are both rich, beautiful and stylish. They belong together. Anyone can see that.'

Amy swallowed. 'Yes. I suppose so. But there do seem to be some differences between them.'

'You mean about the new technology? Oh, that is nothing. A little hitch in the proceedings. She hasn't invited him here to talk about *that*, I assure you, Elsie.'

'It's Amy. So why *has* she invited him here?'

'To propose to him, of course.'

'Oh. These days the women are proposing to the men?'

'Hah! She is as smart as a whip, that one. You know she just got her helicopter licence?'

Amy concentrated on the thick hair. 'Yes, I heard that.'

'Men are like helicopters. You just need to learn which

buttons to push, which levers to pull and, *voilà*, you are flying!' She giggled. 'It will be the wedding of the decade. Help me to put on my housecoat.'

Feeling bruised inside, Amy helped Gerda put on the floral pink geisha gown. Gerda pushed out her monumental bosoms and caressed their curves complacently. 'They are magnificent, aren't they? Yours are all right. Bigger than Lavinia's at least. They're the only thing she lacks—and not for want of trying, either, I might tell you,' she added with a flash of malice.

'I suppose she has all the other advantages a woman could want,' Amy said dully, helping Gerda to tie the sash.

She had to spend most of the rest of the afternoon listening to Gerda boast about her money and her figure—both of which were inherited, apparently, and owed nothing to art. Inside, though, Amy was trying not to let Gerda's gossip-column tittle-tattle weigh too heavily on her soul.

But why should she feel proprietorial about Anton? Just because he had kissed her last night—before that unfortunate interruption? Could she say by that brief moment that he really cared about her? If he went riding with Lavinia—or studying the moonlight with her—it was only business. And *his* business, at that. Wasn't it?

The happy couple returned from their ride looking even more companionable than before. The afternoon had been a hot one, redolent with the smell of herbs and loud with cicadas. Amy had to fight her imagination to stop visualising what might have transpired between them under some gnarled pine tree or in the shade of some olive grove.

She encountered Anton as he was going upstairs to change. His shirt was unbuttoned and among the dark, crisp hair that covered his muscular chest she could see a few torn rosemary leaves.

'I see she's planning to roast you in herbs,' she said tonelessly.

'Roast is right. That's the hottest I've ever been on a horse. How's your day been?'

'Fascinating. I've spent most of it watching Gerda be sick into a Sèvres bowl.'

'That sounds very colourful.'

'You have no idea.'

'You can hardly complain. The poor lady is obviously turning herself inside-out in order to amuse you.'

'Eeww.'

He kissed her cheek tenderly. 'You are a very brave girl. Your gallantry will not be forgotten.'

'There was a young mogul called Zell,' she intoned, 'who smiled as he rode with a belle; they returned from the ride with the mogul inside and the smile on the face of the belle.'

Anton grinned. 'Oh ye of little faith. Wait and see who eats whom.'

But she didn't want either of them to eat the other, she thought with anguish. She wanted everything to be the way it had been before they came here.

But there was no way in the world she could articulate either of those paradoxical thoughts to him. She just had to smile. 'Go get 'em, tiger.'

He hugged her quickly. 'I know this is boring for you. We'll be out of here in a few days. Be patient. You promised!'

Amy pressed her face to his chest, inhaling the delicious smell of his hot skin for a moment, then pushed him away. 'Go and wash. And be sure to pick all the leaves out of your hair, dahling boy.'

At dinner that night, Amy found herself relegated to an even more remote corner of the table. There were extra guests for dinner, mostly quite elderly people, and she was seated on the far side of them. That effectively stopped her from contributing any more unwelcome interpolations into the general conversation—and also prevented her from hearing much of what was said by Anton, Lavinia and the inner circle.

It was a special torture to watch him, from what felt like miles away, apparently having a wonderful time; so handsome when he laughed at Lavinia's sly jokes, so urbane when he spoke. Amy felt more and more like the invisible woman. She shrank into herself, smiling politely at the yarns which the elderly gentleman who was her neighbour seemed to have so many of, but feeling cold and lonely inside.

Once again, she was excluded from the after-dinner fun; everyone went down into Antibes to go to a concert where a famous violinist was performing, but she excused herself, knowing her presence would only irritate Lavinia—who showed no signs of forgiveness—and make it harder for Anton. She felt unwanted, a pariah.

The only other house-guest who stayed was Gerda, who was still feeling fragile. Amy stood her excruciating discussion of her bosom and her bank account until she could bear no more, and crept up to bed.

And though she waited until her poor eyelids grew heavy as lead for Anton to come and kiss her goodnight, he had not returned by 2 a.m. and she fell asleep on the coverlet.

It did not help much when, the next morning at breakfast, Anton told her that he had come into her room very late.

'You were fast asleep,' he smiled. 'Snoring like a lumber mill. So I just kissed you goodnight and left you to get your beauty sleep.'

'Oh, thanks,' she said drily, thinking that kisses didn't count if one was not awake to enjoy them. Nor did it escape her attention that he was dressed to go riding again, long legs encased in jeans and well-worn boots. 'Nice evening?'

'After the concert we went to a cabaret show. It was very dull.'

'Tame, no doubt, compared to your Wanchai strip clubs.'

'Well, the girls are taller. Did Gerda throw up any more?' he asked with interest.

'Unfortunately, the flow has come to an end. But I know everything there is to be known about which bras she pours her boobs into and which banks she pours her billions into.'

'That bad?'

'Worse than you can imagine.'

'Oh, dear.'

'Her money and her mammaries are her only topics of conversation, Anton. If I have to spend another hour in her company, I may strangle her.'

'I promise you, Worthington, you're in line for a medal as soon as we can get away from this morgue.'

'And when will that be? You seem unable to tear yourself away from a certain somebody.'

'Darling, if you think Gerda is bad, you want to try Morticia.'

Amy burst out laughing. 'Oh, that's funny! Gerda says she's planning you to be the next Gomez.'

'Marriage? I doubt that. Lavinia is very happy the way she is.'

'I think she's in love with you,' Amy said, her laughter fading away. 'And she's sexy, clever and sophisticated.'

'So?'

'So, you'd have to have a very good reason to turn her down.'

The smile was more in his eyes than on his lips. 'What if I was only interested in someone else?'

'Who would that be?' she asked, her heart jumping.

'Someone with the face of an angel.'

She was about to reply when a familiar female voice enquired, 'And what is the joke, dear boy? May we share?'

They turned to face the bright eyes and lean brown face of Lavinia. She was once again wearing the jodhpurs and cotton shirt that showed off her figure to such advantage, except that today's shade was peppermint-green.

'Just recalling an old TV show,' Anton said with a smile.

'I never seem to have time to watch television.' Lavinia slapped her kid gloves into her palm. 'Have you had breakfast? Then let's get out on the horses before it gets too hot. There are some absolutely wonderful bridle-paths we can take along the mountainside. And I know a country restaurant where they'll look after the horses for us while we have the most scrummy lunch.'

'Sounds good,' Anton said, with only the faintest hint of weariness in his voice—or was that just his way of pacifying Amy's surging indignation at being left alone all day yet again?

And for the second day in a row, she was treated to the spectacle of Anton and Lavinia riding off into the *maquis*, heads close together.

It all washed over her yet again, that familiar pain at being shut out, unwanted, a sinner not admitted to the golden circle. Her cousins had made her feel like that for most of her adolescence. Now Lavinia Carron was doing it all over again—and it hurt so terribly.

If only Lavinia were a more likeable person, Amy told herself, she would be standing up and cheering at the sight of Anton with a suitable Significant Other at his side.

But Lavinia didn't deserve him!

An appreciative, compassionate woman with the ability to understand Anton's own sad past—that was what he needed. Someone who knew where he had come from and why he was the man he was. Someone who believed in the same things he did and who supported him in his dreams— *that* was what he needed.

Not this rapacious, hard-hearted female who thought only about herself and who surrounded herself with people as tough-natured and selfish as herself. That just wasn't fair.

On the third day of their visit, Lavinia had arranged a cruise along the coast to the Îles de Lérins, the archipelago of islands off Cannes where the Man in the Iron Mask had been incarcerated. Gerda Meyer was now fully recovered from her tummy bug and there was no reasonable excuse to exclude Amy—so she found herself invited to go along. The prospect of finally getting to spend some time with Anton— though hardly alone with him—made her accept, though her better judgement told her to stay home.

The boat, a charter, was a graceful white yacht which picked them up at the port. As they sailed out of the bay towards the islands, a cool breeze picked up, washing away the fierce heat that was already building up.

It was another searing day. Banks of cloud along the horizon promised that the hot weather had to break soon.

The sea was crowded with pleasure boats of all types, though—Amy thought wryly—Lavinia could console herself that hers was the biggest and smartest on the waves.

Lavinia's latest materialisation seemed to be as Bond girl—a very small black bikini which showed her tanned and athletic body, over which she had slung a snow-white nautical jacket and very short white shorts, the ensemble completed with a gold-braided white cap. It would have been ridiculous—if she didn't look so damned good in it.

She was in her element, issuing orders, arranging everything, clearly revelling in being master and commander of the whole ark. Fifteen years ago, Amy thought, Lavinia must have been head girl of some élite college for young ladies.

Tomorrow—thank heavens—she and Anton were leaving for Marseilles and then the flight back to Hong Kong.

That gave Lavinia one more day to clinch the deal, she thought cynically. Unless she was going to wait until the annual general meeting in London at the end of the year. If she was wise, waiting until London was the better plan.

Anton might be tempted by all the wealth and that lean brown body to go with it, but Lavinia probably wanted to be quite sure of her prey.

In her own pink and chocolate Christian Dior bikini and tortoiseshell sunglasses, Amy looked feminine and tranquil. She stayed out of the way, leaning on the polished brass rail and watching the green coastline slip past. At least she was out of that awful stone fortress. The blue sea was purifying and relaxing.

Anton leaned on the rail beside her. 'Your face is peaceful for a change,' he said.

'I love the sea,' she replied.

'Ah, I forgot—a mermaid's natural habitat.'

She smiled. 'I thought I was a monkey.'

'Yes, you're definitely a monkey.'

'Always nice to know one's a monkey.'

'I told you in Hong Kong, the monkey is a very nice sign to be. And monkeys are very good in bed, too.'

'Really? In what way?'

'They know how to enjoy pleasure.'

'And that qualifies someone as being good in bed? Selfishness?'

'I didn't mention selfishness. It's actually just the opposite quality. It's taking delight in being loved.'

'I'm not sure I have that particular monkey quality.'

'I'm doing my best to develop it in you.'

'Lavinia certainly knows how to entertain her guests.'

'Robert left her very wealthy,' he replied. 'She has nothing to do but spend her money in a variety of imaginative ways.'

'You talk as though you don't like her much,' Amy replied, glancing at him. He was wearing only black and yellow Hawaiian baggies. His magnificent physique gleamed in the sun, muscles rippling under his golden skin when he moved. She was so jealous of that body; she hated the way other women looked at him.

'I do like her. But she doesn't always understand that she can't have her way in everything, no matter how rich and clever she is.'

'Yes,' Amy said wryly, 'I can see she's giving you a hard time.'

'She wants me to change direction on the new refineries.'

'Is that what you talk about when you're alone together for hours at a time?' she asked, watching a small sailboat bob past in their wake.

'She seems to think she understands the oil business better than I do,' he said with a smile. 'Robert was happy to sit back and rake in the profits, as you put it the other night. Lavinia has ideas about everything. And with the big stake in the corporation which Robert left her, she can throw her weight around.'

'Could she really cause trouble with other shareholders?'

'She knows a lot of people. And she knows how to get things done. If she persuades enough shareholders that I'm taking the corporation in the wrong direction, there could be big problems.'

'What's the worst that could happen?'

'I could be fired as chief executive officer.'

'But it's your company!' she exclaimed.

He shook his head. 'I own a fifty-one per cent stake. But it's a listed company, and if enough of the shareholders were against me, I would have to step down rather than face a civil war and seeing public confidence disintegrate.'

Amy stared at his face. 'You mentioned buying her out.'

'Yes. If I could persuade her to sell. That's one problem. Another is that Zell is a British company, and under British law, if I buy back shares they have to be immediately cancelled. I can't resell them.'

'What would happen?'

'Well, it's complicated. There would be fewer shares in circulation and so the remaining shares would be more valuable, in theory. But it would cost a lot of money, money that I have earmarked for our expansion in south-east Asia. It would mean delaying my plans for a year, perhaps far longer.'

The Bond girl herself was on deck now, surrounded by her friends. There was a palpable air of excitement about the trim, tanned figure; she looked like a woman who knew exactly where she was going.

'Anton!' she called. 'Darling boy, you're missing the dolphins.'

They both turned. A group of three or four dolphins was indeed swimming alongside the yacht, sleek bodies surging in and out of the waves. It was a thrilling sight. Lavinia Carron's triumphant expression suggested she was personally responsible for the presence of the animals.

On second thoughts, Amy decided gloomily, as Lavinia hooked her arm through Anton's and led him away, the creatures were probably animatronic robots, directed by a remote-control unit in the pocket of Lavinia Carron's very short white shorts.

To avoid the crowds, they sailed to the far side of Île Sainte-Marguerite, the largest of the islands. The yacht moored as near the beach as possible and the dinghy took them ashore.

The white beach was hot underfoot. The whole of the island was covered by a natural forest of Aleppo pine and eucalyptus, whose scented and woven shade offered some shelter from the midday heat.

The weather, however, was now threatening. The fierce heat of the past few days seemed to have charged the atmosphere with violence. A grey haze was in the sky. The endless noise of cicadas was deafening and Amy felt oddly breathless from the heat and the close humidity.

'It's going to storm,' Anton warned.

'No, it's not,' Lavinia said sharply, glancing up at the heavy sky as though daring the heavens to contradict her. 'Breathe deeply, everybody. The eucalyptus is wonderful for the lungs!'

Everyone snorted and sucked the fragrant air obediently. Amy wondered bitterly whether they would stop breathing just as tamely if Lady Carron commanded it.

The plan was that the party should walk through the forest to the port, where they were to have lunch in a restaurant and then visit the Fort Royal, where the Man in the Iron Mask had been incarcerated three centuries ago.

Their hostess led the way.

They set off in a group along the winding, sandy paths through the forest. However it soon became obvious that Lavinia, honed by hours in the gymnasium, had overestimated the physical fitness of her party. Complaining about the heat and the oppressive atmosphere, the less athletic began to lag behind, while Lavinia strode on contemptuously ahead. Within a short while, the party was strung out; and the number of twisting paths became confusing, with no directions to follow. The forest seemed endless, the pine trees identical with one another, each path exactly like all the others.

A rumble of thunder pierced Amy's resentment and released a flood of remorse. She had been walking with Gerda Meyer, who was complaining of the heat, but boredom had driven her to quicken her pace. Now Gerda was nowhere to be seen. Heinz, her husband, was up in the front with Lavinia, obviously believing a footsore wife was not a good enough reason to take his eye off such an important client as Lady Carron.

Amy stopped and retraced her steps. Gerda was as dull a woman as creation had ever put wind in, but Amy felt bad about leaving her to wander the forests alone like a silly, bleating sheep.

Walking back a hundred yards or so, she found no trace of Gerda—or of anyone else. She was completely alone in the stifling, cicada-loud woodland. A glare of lightning was instantly followed by a searing crash of thunder so loud and so close overhead that she almost jumped out of her skin.

A gust of hot wind buffeted her. It was clearly about to storm, as Anton had predicted. Amy looked up at the turgid sky anxiously. Sheltering under a tree was not supposed to be a good idea in an electrical storm, but what if there was nothing *but* trees? Could lightning tell one identical eucalyptus from another?

Another shattering peal of thunder heralded more wind and the first heavy, hot drops of rain. Uncertain what to do, Amy hesitated.

And then the heavens opened and a tempest of rain and wind was unleashed. Blinded by the onslaught, Amy blundered off the path into the relative shelter of the trees. There was no point in searching for Gerda now—she would have to wait until the storm was over.

She snuggled into herself, wishing she were wearing something warmer; the temperature was dropping fast and it was turning cold. Damn Lavinia, Amy thought, huddling up to the rough trunk of a pine tree. She was probably sitting in a café now with a glass of wine, stroking her 'darling boy' and chuckling at the fate of the stragglers.

The storm intensified in violence, thunder rolling from one side of the heavens to the other, the rain lashing down in curtains that made visibility impossible.

And then a tall, dark figure materialised through the rain, heading towards her. Her heart jumped into her throat.

'Anton!'

His beautiful white teeth flashed in a grin as he reached her. He was wearing only his Hawaiian baggies and a cerise waterproof poncho which he spread over both their heads for shelter. His wet face pressed to hers as he gave her an exuberant kiss. 'Remember Borneo?' he greeted her.

'How could I forget? Where did you get the poncho?'

'Bought it in the port. Lavinia and the others are having lunch already. I came back to find you.'

'You sweet man! I was very pleased to see you. I hate thunderstorms.'

'How did you get so far behind?'

'I was walking with poor Gerda but I just had to escape and she got left behind. I hope she isn't drowning.'

'Her natural resources will keep her buoyant.'

She smiled. 'I hope so.' Thunder pealed across the sky, making her snuggle up against him more closely. His naked, muscled torso was dripping with rain but that somehow made him all the more desirable. The deep pink shade of the poncho was so intimate. 'And you left dear Lavinia to come running back to me? Such a noble man!'

'She's being particularly impossible today. Going on and on about the new technology.'

'She's moving in on you, Anton,' Amy said. 'She wants to show you how knowledgeable she is. What an asset she would be as a wife. And all this lavish entertainment she's laying on—it's designed to show you the wonderful life you could have together.'

'We spend all our time together arguing, Amy.'

'That's the stick to go with the carrot. She's demonstrating that it makes sense to join forces with her. She's chosen you, can't you see that? Fate has thrown twenty per cent of your corporation into her lap. You are an engineering and business genius, the handsomest man in the world according to *Vogue*, and just plain the most eligible bachelor in sight. She's made marrying you her life's mission—and what Lavinia wants, Lavinia gets.'

His deep blue eyes were watching her face with a

strangely quizzical expression. 'I had no idea you felt that way about me.'

'Oh, come on!' she exclaimed restlessly, laying her palm on his powerful naked chest. 'With her twenty per cent and your fifty-one per cent, you'll never have to worry about boardroom battles again. I'm surprised she hasn't spelled it out just as clearly as that.'

'Perhaps she's hoping I would take her without her twenty per cent,' he said gently.

'And would you?' she asked directly.

'I'm much more interested in all these compliments you've just paid me—that I'm handsome, a genius…and an eligible bachelor.'

'You know all that,' she said impatiently. 'Modesty is not one of your virtues.'

'Maybe not. But I'm still somewhat surprised to hear all that coming out of your mouth.'

'Don't be silly,' she retorted. 'Why should you be surprised?'

'I had the impression you don't think very much of me,' he replied, still looking at her with that odd expression.

She gaped. 'Don't think very much of you? What made you think that?'

'Well, every time I try to touch you, you push me away— or run like a rabbit. It's plain you have some violent aversion to being close to me.'

Amy was dumbfounded for a moment. 'Anton, not wanting to become your latest mistress doesn't mean I don't admire you passionately as a human being.'

His eyelids drooped. 'Ah. I'm a genius, but physically unattractive?'

'This is insanity,' she said, half laughing in perplexity. 'Of course you're not unattractive! Haven't I just said you're the handsomest man in the world?'

'According to *Vogue*.'

'And according to every other female who lays eyes on you!'

'Including you?'

He had fenced her neatly into a corner. 'Yes, Anton,' she said quietly, 'including me.'

Her palm was still resting on his chest. He leaned close to her, his warm bare skin touching hers. 'And so you run because…'

'I told you already. Because I'm not going to be your toy.'

He brushed her wet, golden hair with his lips. 'I'm confused. What am I—nice guy or monster?'

'I never said you were a monster. I never said you were a nice guy, either!'

'So what am I?'

'You're a hunter,' she replied.

'A hunter of what?'

'Of whatever you want. Of success. Of women.'

He laughed quietly. 'I thought you'd just been trying to explain how Lavinia was hunting *me*?'

'Yes, that must be a new experience for you. It's usually you doing the stalking.'

'So you think I'm stalking you?'

'Yes!'

'So I can jump on you…and eat you up?'

A rumble of thunder prevented her from replying; and then it was too late. Anton was kissing her with the passion of a man who wanted her desperately. She clung to him, her hungry fingers running across the contours of his naked torso, nails digging in, pulling him closer to her.

Their tongues were tasting one another. Amy's eyes were tight shut but she had never been so aware of who she was kissing—not some faceless figure in a fantasy, but Anton, the man she was growing to love so helplessly, the man she respected and cherished above all others.

She pressed her stomach against his, intoxicated by the naked contact between them. She wanted to tell him how much he meant to her, how frantic she was for his touch. All her caution was melting away like a sugar-cone castle in this tropical downpour.

And then she became aware of a bleating sound, like a lost and very bedraggled sheep.

They turned to see Gerda Meyer staring at them. Her yellow hair hung down in soaked sheets in front of her face but there was no doubt that she could see what was happening perfectly.

'What are you doing?' she demanded in outrage, eyes popping.

'We came to look for you,' Amy said. 'We thought you were lost.'

'I *was* lost,' Gerda said bitterly. 'Everybody just abandoned me. But now it is I who have found *you*, it seems!'

Anton raised an eyebrow at Amy in amused commentary. But Amy did not return the smile. There was no question but that Gerda would report what she had seen to Lavinia— and a disenchanted Lavinia could only spell a great deal of trouble for Anton in the future.

The rain was not yet easing off, but it seemed preferable to brave the thunderbolts rather than try and fit three discomfited people under the one pink poncho, so they walked along the path to the port. Anton tried to hold Amy's hand, but she pulled away from him, anxious not to give Gerda any further ammunition. 'Please don't,' she whispered. 'It's not worth it!'

'Amy, don't pull away from me!'

'Not in front of her! Lavinia can be very bad news for you, Anton. I could never forgive myself if I made things worse for you.'

Gerda, for her part, was evidently bursting for a little private chat with Amy.

She took Amy's arm and drew her aside with a face like thunder. 'What did you think you were doing back there?' she hissed imperiously.

'We were just sheltering from the rain,' Amy said, attempting a desperate defence.

'You were practically devouring him! I have never seen a woman kiss a man so shamelessly as you were doing! Did I not tell you that Lavinia and Anton are going to be married?'

'Lavinia may have told you that that is her plan,' Amy retorted before wiser council silenced her, 'but she cannot speak for Anton!'

'You little fool,' Gerda snapped. 'Do you want to ruin him? Do you really think he could be serious about *you*, a nobody, a junior employee? Do you think you are the first secretary who has fallen in love with him?'

The words bit into her heart like an axe. 'No, I don't think that,' she said quietly.

'The last one was so crazy about him it was embarrassing to everybody,' Gerda went on, shaking the dripping hair out of her eyes. 'You are even worse, getting in the way all the time, like a badly behaved child! All he wants from you is quick sex, can't you understand that? You can have no idea how much trouble you are causing!'

'I don't want to get in anybody's way.' Wisdom made Amy bite her tongue and refrain from saying anything further. The last thing she wanted was to harm Anton. Whatever he wanted from her, and whatever his plans with Lavinia, she cared about him enough not to wish him harmed in any way.

Gerda's eyes narrowed. 'I see now! You think that once they are married, he will install you as his mistress in some lacquered palace in Hong Kong!'

'What?'

Gerda chuckled. 'So, you are not so stupid as I thought!

A business wife in France and a pleasure wife in Hong Kong? Oh, yes, he is man enough for that.'

'Unfortunately, I'm not woman enough for such an arrangement,' Amy replied icily.

'Come, come. You needn't play the grand lady with me, *chère*. I am a woman of the world. And I know men like Anton Zell. They want it all—and they always get to have it all.'

Anton Zell can have it all. The fact that she herself had used exactly those words to Anton a few days earlier did not escape Amy. She gritted her teeth. 'I'm not a grand lady.'

'No, but you are not stupid, either.' Gerda's shrewd glance contained a new respect. 'Lavinia is a grand lady. She has money and power. But you have something else, something she will never have. Play your cards right, and it will work. As long as you don't get in Lavinia's way, she may even tolerate you!'

'Tolerate?'

'Empresses sometimes tolerate a concubine—or two,' Gerda said with a malicious smile.

Amy hurried on, leaving the older woman behind. But Gerda's vicious words were stuck in her heart like daggers.

The rest of the afternoon was dark and rainy. Amy could not be sure at what point Gerda Meyer spilled the beans to Lavinia—Lavinia was far too socially accomplished to give any great outward show of outrage—but there was no question that the beans had been spilled. The way Lavinia behaved as though Amy didn't even exist confirmed that.

The downpour and several of the party having been marooned in the forest made for a somewhat subdued evening meal, punctuated by sniffs and sneezes. Amy made sure she avoided both Anton and Lavinia Carron; right now, she didn't want to be alone with either of them.

It rained and blew all night. It seemed to Amy, in bed early, that the dawn would never come. She tried not to think about what might be passing between Anton and Lavinia as the lightning flashed and the thunder rumbled. Anton had said things about Lavinia that showed he was not blinded by her wealth and magnetism. But then, a man did not have to be in love to marry.

A man like Anton needed a strong wife, not a sugar-plum fairy. He might reckon that marriage to Lavinia would give him enough power to accomplish just about anything in life and that it was not necessary that she be a saint into the bargain.

And as for that searing kiss in the forest—he probably reasoned that he could pick many flowers along the way without losing sight of his main goal.

With these and similar thoughts she tormented herself, feeling more wretched and creating uglier monsters until the grey dawn brought relief and she could drag herself into the shower and try to rinse away the pain.

The breakfast-room did not appear to be a very joyous place when she went down. On the other hand, both Anton and Lavinia seemed to be in normal mood and were talking to one another quite cheerfully. Anton wanted to make an early start, so the leave-taking was mercifully brief.

The bags were soon loaded into the car beside the fountain with the snarling lions. Lavinia bestowed a kiss on Anton's mouth that seemed warm enough. Then she turned to Amy, as though suddenly Amy had become visible again. She smiled thinly and said only five words, in a voice so quiet that nobody else heard:

'Don't get in my way.'

Amy said nothing in reply, but the look in Lavinia Carron's eyes stayed with her for a long time—well until they were on the motorway back to Marseilles. The sky appeared bruised and there was still a steady rain falling, drumming on the canvas hood of the Mercedes.

'Stormy night,' Amy said at last, breaking the silence.

'Yes,' Anton replied.

'Well,' she demanded, unable to bear the suspense any longer, 'what happened last night? Did she pop the question?'

Anton burst out laughing. 'Of course she didn't pop the question, you silly girl.'

'Then she'll be waiting until the chairman's report in London,' Amy said decisively. 'She's sweetened you up with boat rides and good food and fabulous entertainment this time. Next time, she'll be carrying the big stick.'

He glanced at her with amused eyes. 'You think she's after my hide?'

'Wait and see,' Amy said gloomily. 'Just wait and see.'

CHAPTER NINE

BY THE end of September they were in Vietnam.

Amy was getting used to the great Asian cities, with their vast metropolitan centres and immense populations. Saigon's centre was featureless and busy. But once out in the suburbs, it still had the feel of a town with a heart. Instead of the districts of featureless apartment blocks that made up the suburbs of other Asian metropolises, she found charming, dilapidated streets of vintage old buildings that sprawled along the banks of the river.

It was rather like stepping back in time. The streets swarmed with bicycles and scooters. The cars all tended to be vintage models. Even the company car that picked them up from the airport was a forty-year-old Peugeot, rather than the battleship limos of richer cities.

'What a dreamy place!' she sighed happily to Anton in the car. 'Aren't we supposed to call it Ho Chi Minh City?'

'People are tending to call it that now, but it's taken a few years for the name to stick.'

'I love it, whatever it's called,' she said, gazing out of the window. 'It's very different from Singapore or Hong Kong. Some parts look like bits of Paris that have been somehow dumped in Asia and left to soften!'

'Even the colours are different,' he agreed. It was true; the delicate yellows, pinks and lime-greens of the buildings blended in beautifully with one another along the tree-lined boulevards. 'And notice how clean the streets are. The devastation of the war has made the Vietnamese very conscious of their environment. That's one of the reasons I like dealing with them.'

116

They were not going to be staying in a hotel in Saigon, but in a company villa which the Zell Corporation had bought in the suburbs. She was curious to see what it looked like, since someone at Zell in Hong Kong had told her it was the most beautiful house he had ever been in—in fact, he had become quite dreamy-eyed at the memory.

Their car passed through tall, ornate iron gates and pulled up in a cobbled courtyard. Two maids, delicate Vietnamese girls dressed in black and white uniforms, came out to greet them and help them with their bags.

'This is exquisite,' Amy said with delight as she walked through the house. Indeed, it was more of a small palace than a villa, an intoxicating mixture of French empire and Forbidden City, with rococo mouldings and Oriental antiques, Buddhist silk hangings and dim oil paintings. Her bedroom was vast, with a four-poster bed in the centre of the room, draped with diaphanous voile.

The smiling maid opened the glass doors that led onto the garden. Amy stepped outside, bemused. The walled garden was huge, shaded by great trees with glossy leaves. She could see large and ancient bronze urns meditating among the shrubbery. In the centre was a pond, its surface covered with the pink and yellow flowers and emerald-coloured pads of water lilies. In the still water beneath, crimson and saffron fish drifted in a dream.

She sat on the edge of the pond and trailed her fingers in the water. She gazed at the strawberry-pink house. It belonged to a different era, with empire balconies and arches. Cream marble columns held up the portico. The windows and parapets were picked out in the same pale marble. It had been impeccably restored, and given a Riviera flourish, complete with pink stucco and striped awnings.

Anton came to join her. He had changed into jeans and a plain white shirt. He sat beside her on the wall. 'Like it?' he asked.

'I don't know what to say. It's the most beautiful house I've ever seen.'

'It belonged to a member of the French civil government. After the war it was expropriated. I bought it from the Vietnamese government five years ago.'

'You have wonderful taste,' she said.

'Some day I might come and live here,' he said. 'At least part of the year, anyway. I have an ongoing love affair with Vietnam.'

'Then I'll try and love it too.' She smiled at him. The long shadow cast by Lavinia Carron had disappeared from between them. London was weeks away and she was determined to forget about it until the time came.

'Come,' Anton said as a gong sounded, 'they want us to have lunch now.'

The meal was served in the long dining-room from ornate silver tureens, and was bewilderingly delicious. It started with little crab parcels fried in pastry wrappings, proceeded through a succession of elaborate dishes she couldn't even begin to identify—sometimes it seemed to her she was eating French haute cuisine and then the next bite would take her to China—and concluded with a frozen dessert that had a taste that eluded her utterly.

'It's durian ice cream,' Anton informed her. 'Durians are those strange, spiky fruit you see on roadside stalls. The taste is delicious but they heat up the stomach, and the smell is—well, unique. Turning them into ice cream solves the problem.'

'I've never had anything more exotic,' she said honestly. 'I think that was the best meal of my life.'

'You're starting to see why I love Vietnam,' he smiled. 'We'd better get out to the site. They're expecting us.'

The refinery was being built to the east of Saigon, on the coast. The drive there took them through vast rice fields that glittered in the sun, fed by an endless watery network of irrigation canals, waterways and rivers. The countryside was so inextricably mingled with water, indeed, that the commonest means of transport to be seen were sailing vessels of every type imaginable.

They reached the coast after driving through hills of alternating jungle and sugar-cane plantations. The refinery was situated in the ceremoniously named Vung Tao Con Dau Special Zone and it was in the middle of an area of outstanding natural beauty. The Zone, however, was carefully landscaped so as not to spoil the scenery. Rolling green hills surrounded it; a few miles below, the resort town of Vung Tao spread out along a snowy white crescent of beach that reminded her of a huge slice of watermelon—if the sea had been pink instead of deep blue.

The Vung Tao refinery was almost complete. It was one of Anton's most ambitious projects, a plant designed to refine used lubricating oil from the automotive industry and turn it back into something pristine. In an economy like Vietnam's, it was a project that could save millions on oil imports and encourage growth. It represented the kind of thinking that she most admired in Anton—his ability to find solutions for less wealthy clients, saving money and preserving the environment.

Even the colours of the plant seemed positive, a mass of scarlet, green and bright yellow piping that somehow made her think of a huge children's game. The Vietnamese engineers could not have been more hospitable or charming; this was a country of exquisite manners.

Two phases of the plant were running already and they were able to watch the process at work. Wearing the obligatory hard hats, she and Anton walked the length of the plants, the engineers and the interpreters talking enthusiastically about the results they were obtaining.

'Notice something?' Anton asked her, pointing to the

towers. 'No flames. Most refineries burn off waste from chimneys, releasing poisons into the air. We've eliminated that.'

'It's a remarkable achievement,' she said.

In the quality-control lab, a smiling assistant brought two glass beakers for them to compare—one containing black sludge that was the starting point, the other containing a clear golden oil that was the finished product.

'It's hard to believe this can turn into this,' Amy commented.

'Smell the used oil,' Anton commanded.

She obeyed, and wrinkled her nose. 'Not nice. It smells like dirty old engines.'

'Now smell the clean oil.'

'Nectar,' she grinned, amused by his earnestness. 'I think I'll put some behind my ears.'

'Well, at least you can put it in your engine. It's cheaper than imported oil by a long way and it solves the problem of disposing of dirty oil.'

'All our tests on this oil have shown that it meets industry standards, Mr Zell,' added one of the Vietnamese engineers, an older man with gold-rimmed glasses and a white moustache. 'We are very pleased with the results!'

Anton smiled and nodded. But when he caught Amy's gaze, he waggled an eyebrow suggestively. She knew he was hoping to sell more such plants to the Vietnamese and this was a very encouraging sign.

Indeed, as they left the plant some three hours later, he was in a more upbeat mood than she had seen him in for days. 'The man with the gold-rimmed spectacles and the moustache is no ordinary engineer,' he told her. 'He's a senior official in the government's energy programme. It looks like we'll be getting those new orders soon.'

'I'm so happy for you.'

He grinned at her. 'It ain't bad. Hey. Want to go to the beach before we head home?'

'That would be wonderful!'

It was late afternoon and golden sunlight was washing the coastline. The day had been very hot. She felt nothing would be nicer than a visit to the sea.

The driver took them through Vung Tao to a section of beach that was absolutely deserted, more beautiful than any tourist brochure could depict. White sand stretched out for miles, lapped by a gentle sea. Sea birds wheeled overhead. It was heavenly.

Leaving the driver with the car, she and Anton took off their shoes, rolled up their trousers, and wandered along the beach side by side.

'I can see why you love this place,' she said to him. 'It's a slice of paradise. And your refinery is helping to protect it.'

He stooped and picked up a shell. 'Politics have kept their economy from developing the way other Asian tigers have done. Now they can choose their own path to wealth.'

He handed her the shell. It was pink, ribbed on one side and pearly on the inside. 'It's perfect.'

He looked into her face. Here by the sea, his eyes were the deepest blue imaginable. 'It's been a long, hot day. I feel like swimming. Join me?'

'I left my bikini back at the villa! I didn't think we'd be swimming!'

'Don't you ever do anything spontaneous?' he asked.

She looked at the inviting waves longingly, then at the car, barely visible in the distant haze. 'In my underwear? And be wet and sandy all the way back to Saigon?'

'Well, as an engineer, I can tell you that there are multiple solutions to this problem. You can take off your dress, swim in your underwear and go home wearing a dry dress but with no underwear. Or you can take off your underwear, swim in your dress, and go home wearing dry underwear. Or you can take off both your dress and your underwear, swim as Mother Nature intended, and go home in a dry dress *and* underwear.' He laughed softly at her expression. 'I'll leave you to work it out, Worthington. I promise not to look at you, whatever you decide. You shall be as a maiden invisible unto mine eyes.'

'Or I could not swim at all,' she said in a small voice.

He sighed wearily. 'And stay hot and sticky. It's your decision.' He was already unbuttoning his shirt. She looked away quickly. The beach was deserted. She hunted in vain for a chaste rock to disrobe behind.

When she looked back at Anton, he was walking down to the water. He had kept his briefs on, she saw with relief. His muscular, tanned body slipped with barely a splash into the blue water.

The way he'd said *it's your decision* had stung her. She was so afraid that his patience would finally run out with her behaviour—with what he probably saw as her ridiculous prudery.

She stripped off her dress and ran down to the water in her pale blue underwear.

The sea was deliciously cool. She laughed out loud with the delight of feeling the day's heat and grime vanish. She swam out from the shore, her body buoyed on the gentle swells of the South China Sea. What a heavenly place! This was surely the very beach that featured in all those holiday brochures, and somehow never seemed to exist in real life. 'Anton?' she called. 'Where are you?'

Tanned arms closed around her waist. She gasped and squirmed, but his muscular body was far too strong for her.

'You scared the life out of me,' she spluttered, turning to face him.

'Aren't you glad you took the plunge?' he said, laughing.

'It's wonderful!'

'For a moment I thought you were going to sit there on the beach, all forlorn, like Miss Muffet.'

'Don't laugh at me. Men can always strip off and jump into the sea. In case you hadn't noticed, I'm not a man.'

Anton was still holding on to her arms. He drew her towards him so that his face, the most beautiful male face she had ever seen, was close to hers. 'What makes you imagine,' he said in an intimate murmur, 'that I haven't noticed you're a woman?'

'Perhaps I phrased that wrong,' she rejoined in a whisper that was almost as intimate. 'I meant to say *a lady*.'

'Is there a difference between a woman and a lady, Miss Worthington?'

'A lady knows how to behave!'

'Whereas a woman knows how to have fun?'

'That's a typical male attitude. That's what men always say when they want a woman to abandon her principles. *It's only a bit of fun*. But somehow, the fun is all on your side— and the pain is on ours.'

'Not all men are like that,' he said.

She searched his eyes, which were a deep indigo, for the truth. 'I haven't seen any exceptions,' she whispered.

'I'm an exception.' His mouth brushed her eyelids. Her skin, flushed with the sun, felt a million times more sensitive than normal. Her fingers curled, nails digging into his muscular shoulders as she offered her half-open mouth to his.

He claimed it as possessively as if only he, in all the world, had that right. She pressed to him in the cool water, the soft peaks of her breasts thrusting against his chest, covered only by her flimsy bra. It was a kiss more passionate than anything she had ever known. Like a roller coaster thundering down a slope out of control, then swooping up into the air, leaving her stomach behind, so that her heart lurched.

'Anton,' she whispered, 'what are we doing?'

'Isn't it obvious?' He smiled. That the kiss had ignited his passions too was obvious by the deep blue fire in his eyes.

'We can't ever be like this together!' she said.

'Isn't this what we've both wanted, since the moment we met?'

'Perhaps you've wanted it,' she said shakily, 'but God knows I've tried to avoid it in every way I could.'

'Even that day on the island?'

'Even then.'

'What are you so afraid of?' he demanded.

She touched her lips with her fingertips. His kiss had left them throbbing, almost bruised. 'I'm afraid of what you do to me.'

'I thought you wanted that as much as I did.'

'Of course I did. That doesn't mean it's sensible!'

'Or prudent, or moral, or safe?'

'None of those things!' She floated away from him on the billowing waves. 'You said we were doing this to cool off.'

He shook his head wryly. 'You're cool, all right.'

Despite her flippancy, Amy was in anguish. When he'd kissed her like that, her whole body had responded in a way she couldn't control. Even now, she was aching in perilous ways. Her legs felt weak, there was electricity pulsing through her breasts and loins.

She knew exactly what the game was. The cooler she was, the more she aroused the hunter in him. From the start he had seen her as a potential conquest. And now she was not going to be the one that had got away.

As for her own feelings, she was caught in a paradox. She was wildly attracted to him, adored him, but she could not go through another Martin McCallum situation again. Her heart had been damaged almost beyond repair. She was desperately trying to save what was left.

Yet when she felt Anton's desire for her, her whole body sang with joy. She wanted him to see her as a woman, but not as a lover. She wanted this to go on forever just the way it was.

They emerged from the water as the sun was starting to set. She reached up to squeeze the water out of her hair. 'That was lovely,' she said to him, smiling.

His face had changed. He was looking at her body as though in awe. 'Mercy,' he whispered huskily. 'You are so sexy.'

Dismayed, she saw that her flimsy underwear had been rendered all but transparent by the water. She was concealing few secrets from him. 'I'd better get dressed,' she said unsteadily.

'Amy, you're the most desirable woman I've ever seen,' he said quietly. 'I wish I could understand you.'

'I wish you could understand me, too,' she said in a sad voice. Standing there, his magnificent male body still streaming with seawater, he was like some ocean god wanting to claim his bride. If only he knew how she longed to throw herself into his arms!

'There are so many fabulous beaches on this coast,' he said. 'We could go somewhere else tomorrow. Take a picnic, spend the day.'

'The day? The whole *day*? How could you possibly afford to take all day off from your mighty works, oh master? You need to get your priorities straight!'

'You're right,' he replied. 'My priorities have been upside-down for a long time.'

'Meaning?' she asked curiously.

'Meaning I've been neglecting the truly important things in life.'

'Which are…?'

'This,' he replied succinctly.

'What do you mean by *this*?' she demanded.

His deep blue eyes met hers. 'The beach. A sunny day. The woman of my dreams in wet underwear.'

She looked at herself. Her nipples were plainly visible as strawberry peaks under the lacy bra. 'Are those the truly important things in life? This is the latest wisdom from Workaholics Anonymous?'

He laughed. 'Well, maybe it's time I took the cure.'

'Well, I don't have billions to rest my laurels on. I am a working girl. I have to take care of your calls, Mr Zell.' As if on cue, the satellite phone started to buzz from its nest in her dress. 'I'd better answer that.'

He held her wrist, restraining her. 'Let the damned thing ring.'

She met his smiling eyes. 'Are you serious? About tomorrow?'

'Very serious,' he said. He drew her to him and kissed her forehead. His body brushed hers, muscled and smooth. Now her heart accelerated like a locomotive, screaming *danger, danger*.

'You can't kiss me!'

'Why not?'

'You're the boss, I'm the employee. I'm a cat, you're a dog. It doesn't work like that!'

He was amused. He drew a line down her nose with his fingertip. 'Maybe we're both cats, and we just don't know it. Or both dogs.'

'Well, thank you so much for calling me a dog,' she said with mock-indignation.

'You're not a dog,' he said gently. 'There isn't a more beautiful woman than you in the whole wide world.'

She wanted him so much in that moment that it was all she could do to stop herself from throwing her arms round his neck and devouring that erotic, maddening mouth.

They dressed and walked back along the beach to the car holding hands.

CHAPTER TEN

THEY ate their evening meal at opposite ends of the table, the room lit by two candelabra, which cast a rosy light on their faces. It was the most romantic meal, and Amy's stomach was already populated with a horde of butterflies, so she could hardly taste the exotic dishes that proceeded from the kitchen, one after another.

It was a sultry, still evening. When the coffee had been drunk, Anton rose from his chair. 'I have a present for you.'

Half expecting a repetition of the jade-bangle episode, Amy smiled nervously. 'Really?'

'It was in the house when I bought it. I think it's perfect for you.' He took something from the mantelpiece and handed it to her.

Amy inspected the thing curiously. It was a little wooden box, its sides made of stretched gauze, with four little feet. The lid could be fastened shut and had a hook so that the box could be suspended. It was charming in its simplicity but she had no idea what it was.

'What is it? A little cage for something?'

'It comes from Japan. It's a firefly lantern. Come, let me show you.'

He picked up a painted paper fan and led her out into the garden. Amy exclaimed in delight; the warm darkness was dotted with dozens of tiny wandering lights. They drifted over the pond, especially, their bright glow reflected in the still water. 'That's so beautiful!'

'Let me show you what to do.' He opened the lid of the lantern, then used the fan to deftly tap one of the luminous insects into it. 'It's easy. Try.'

Gingerly, she took the things from him and started hunting the nearest firefly. It was not quite as easy as Anton had made it look. After several wild swats, she learned how to coax the little creature into the box. She snapped the lid shut triumphantly. 'There!'

'Very good,' he said with soft irony, sitting on the wall of the pond. 'Let's see if you can catch enough to make your lantern useful.'

'It's not as easy as it looks,' she said.

'This is what young Asian women used to do on warm evenings,' he said. 'Before radio, before television.'

She tapped another firefly into the box. 'Got you! And what did the young Asian men do?'

'They watched the young women, of course. It's one of the prettiest sights in the world.'

'I hope I don't fall in the pond,' she said, concentrating on a particularly brilliant insect that was drifting languidly over the lily pads.

'At least you'll have a change of underwear handy,' he said ironically.

'You must think me an awful ninny,' Amy said, snapping another firefly into the gauze box.

'No,' he replied. 'I think you're very complicated. I try to see into your mind but usually I can't. I know that there are things that bother you. But I don't know why.'

Amy was silent.

'One of the things that seem to bother you,' he went on after a silence, 'is Marcie. I don't know why. I don't know what you've been told. But it certainly wasn't the truth.'

She had captured another two fireflies in her box and now she stood very still. 'What is the truth?'

'Up until now, I've considered that the truth wasn't mine to tell. But what I've started to feel for you overrides that. So I'm going to tell you what I have no right to tell you.'

She stepped down from the wall and sat beside him, the

little box glimmering like a fairy lantern in her hands. She watched the trapped insects flitting to and fro. 'Go on.'

'Marcie was a fine personal assistant, but she had a drug problem. She'd had it before she came to me. When she started working for me, she was clean. She managed to conceal it during the interview process and she never told me about it. But the stress of the job began to tell on her and after a while it was obvious there was something wrong. I found out what it was. She was using cocaine heavily. I should have fired her then, but I didn't. Instead, I got involved. Not sexually, but in her problem. I made her go for treatment. I gave her leave so she could do rehab, get herself together again. And then I took her back. I told her I would fire her if she went back on drugs. I thought I had solved her problem. It was a mistake.'

'People say she was deeply in love with you,' Amy said in a low voice.

'I think that was part of the problem. That was part of what made it so hard for her to carry on. Without drugs, I mean. But there was nothing I could do for her. I didn't return her feelings. But I don't flatter myself that the problem was just that. I think she'd been an addict for a long time, and the pressure of the job made it worse. Within a few months, I could tell she was using again. She made bad mistakes, did sloppy things that put people at risk. I made her go for a medical. The blood test said it all. So I fired her.'

'She went to Switzerland?'

'Yes. I paid for her to attend an advanced new drug-rehab clinic near Zurich. She's still there. I hope she works her life out. But that's up to her now.'

Amy looked at her box. 'My lantern is pretty,' she said in a quiet voice, 'but it didn't shed much light.'

'Some lanterns are just for looking at,' he said.

'I couldn't see past the end of my own nose,' she said,

mourning her own emotional misjudgements. 'I'm so sorry I said what I did. I thought—'

'What did you think?' he demanded as she broke off.

'Nothing,' she muttered. It was certainly better that he did not know the dark thoughts that had been going through her mind. It was just as well the firefly lantern shed such a dim light; her face was scarlet with humiliation. She wanted to run away from Anton right now, run and not stop until she was a hundred miles away from his presence.

As if sensing her thoughts, he rose. 'I'm going to turn in, Worthington. Coming?'

'I think I'll sit out here in the cool for a little while longer,' she said thickly.

'Don't stay out too late. I think you got a touch of the sun today. You need sleep. Goodnight.'

'Goodnight, Anton.'

There was no goodnight kiss. He walked back into the house. Amy sat turning the glowing lantern in her hands, her mind occupied with many thoughts, not all of them happy ones. She had rushed to judge Anton by her own lights. The fact that she had been so far from the truth said more about her than it did about Anton.

They had rushed to judge her in just the same way. She'd had no defence against the wagging tongues, the sneering eyes of those who thought themselves so much better than she. It had hurt so much.

Now she had done exactly the same thing to Anton, the one person in all the world she most cared about. Did he guess the way her thoughts had run? Had he heard the rumours that the silly nurse in Hong Kong was spreading?

The first thing she would do when she got back, she vowed, was go to her and tell her just how wrong she was. She did not need to give away Marcie's secrets—just tell a foolish gossip how harmful her speculations were.

The little fairy lights revolved restlessly in her lantern.

She opened the lid and shook their prison gently. Like a shower of sparks, the glowing creatures spiralled upwards and dispersed into the dark, velvety Vietnamese night.

She had not believed that Anton was serious about taking the next day off; but she felt his hand shake her gently awake very early the next morning, and struggled upright to accept the coffee and brioche—both authentically French and steaming hot—that he had brought her.

'Rise and shine,' he said, smiling at her tousle-haired confusion. 'We're going to the seaside.'

Within half an hour they were driving through the early-morning traffic out of the city. This time there were just the two of them in the large and dignified old Peugeot. The chauffeur, too, was getting a day off.

'You seem to be having fun driving this old lady,' she commented, sitting sideways in her seat to watch him. 'Isn't it rather a come-down after your pocket rocket in Hong Kong?'

'It's a change of pace, not a come-down,' he said, grinning. 'I'm taking your advice, and getting my life in order.'

She raised one eyebrow. 'Is that what I said?'

'You told me to get my priorities straight.'

'Where are we going, anyway?' she demanded.

'To Bai An,' he said. 'It's one of my favourite places on the coast. We can hire a boat for twenty dollars and tour the islands.'

Bai An was like a landscape out of a dream. When they arrived at the little bay an hour or so later, the early-morning mist was starting to lift. The white crescent of beach was walled with crumbling cliffs. The glassy water of the bay was dotted with innumerable small islands, some no more than weathered spires of rock, others large hummocks covered with tropical vegetation.

'I've never seen anything as beautiful as this,' Amy said honestly. 'I'm not dreaming, am I?'

'I'll pinch you if you like,' he invited, parking the venerable Peugeot near a collection of wooden boats. They got out and Anton negotiated with one of the fishermen to rent a boat. The vessel he chose was a comfortable-looking wooden sampan with a high prow, on which two eyes had been painted.

'What an adorable boat,' she smiled as he reached out his hands to pull her on deck.

Anton helped Amy aboard, his strong arms lifting her as though she weighed no more than a feather. 'You approve?'

'I'm honoured to climb aboard!'

The sampan was in good condition. Her woodwork wore a deep, lustrous varnish. On her high, elegant transom, a little awning offered shade. The sails that were so neatly furled against her mast were a faded red. Down below, her engine was already rumbling like a contented cat.

The owner threw the mooring rope to Anton. With a word of thanks and a wave, Anton took the wheel and began steering the boat out to the islands.

Lost in the joy of the occasion, Amy curled up in the seat and just drank it in. With expert ease, Anton steered them through the maze of smaller islands and fishing boats and out to the larger islands.

A pair of white cranes flapped lazily across their path. Amy had been in the East long enough to know that the birds were auspicious. It was going to be a good day!

An hour later, she was in a state of bliss. If she had any thought in her mind at all, it was that she had seldom been so happy. Not since her early childhood. It had been the most lovely of mornings.

She had changed into her bikini and was lazing on the deck, watching the islands drift by through dreamy eyes.

The same sun that was baking her semi-naked limbs was making each island glow in shades of emerald and gold. Coconut palms and flowering shrubs hung from the craggy rocks. Their sampan was weaving her elegant way through a world where sea surrounded rock and rock surrounded sea, as if in a beautiful dream. They had all this beauty to themselves. It was as if the whole of nature were theirs on this perfect morning, and they its only inheritors.

Anton cut the engines and hauled up the red sail, its wooden battens making it look like a butterfly's wing or a red leaf. They were making their gentle way on wind power alone. It was wonderful to feel the sweet surge of the boat beneath her, knowing that Anton was at the wheel. She glanced at him now. He had stripped to his swimming trunks. The breeze was ruffling his dark hair.

He was the most magnificent man she had ever seen. There was no way to deny that. His body was perfect, not heavily muscled, yet carved as if by a master sculptor. Success had not changed that lean frame of his one iota; she could see the powerful muscles shifting under his bronzed skin, and his belly was flat and taut. His long legs, braced against the movement of the boat, were those of a long-distance runner.

She had been comparing all the men she had known to Anton Zell, she realised. None measured up. No man had ever been as intelligent, as amusing, as physically beautiful.

As if sensing her thoughts, Anton glanced her way and met her eyes.

'I thought you were asleep.'

'Just daydreaming.'

He pointed to the island ahead of them. 'That is Hon Giang,' he said. 'It's bigger than the rest and it has its own private beach. We'll stop there and swim. We'll be there in a few minutes.' He smiled that heart-stopping smile of his. 'You look just like a sleepy cat.'

'Purr.'

'Hungry?'

'Yes,' she said, half-surprised at the sudden rumble in her own stomach.

'We'll have our picnic on the island. Come here. I want you to see the beach as we come into the cove.'

She joined him behind the wheel. He slid a strong arm around her shoulders and drew her close to his side. She could not stop the sensuous shudder from running down her spine. His skin was hot and silky against her. The close contact melted her insides so that she felt like a dab of butter on a nice brown piece of toast, just oozing deep into him… She had a sudden vision of the fireflies, released from their prison, escaping into the humid darkness last night.

'There,' he said. 'Look.'

He turned the sampan into the cove. It was completely deserted. A fringe of palm trees shaded the snow-white sands of the beach. The water, as clear and still as glass, was turquoise blue. Gulls wheeled lazily overhead. Apart from the birds, everything here belonged to them.

'This is the loveliest place!'

'Yes.' His arm had slid down around her waist. His fingers caressed her skin gently. 'Amazing, isn't it?'

Somehow, though she was not aware of doing so, she had rested her head on his broad shoulder. His hot skin burned her cheek. 'I wish this moment would last for ever,' she whispered.

He must have heard her soft voice above the murmur of the sea, because his arm tightened around her. 'It doesn't have to end,' he said.

'Everything has to end.'

'No.' He kissed her neck gently. 'Not everything.'

'Anton, stop,' she pleaded. She was feeling dizzy. 'We've been through this before!'

'And we will go through it again. Until you accept me.'

She looked at him for a moment, and it was like looking over the edge of a high building. It would be so terribly easy to just let go and fall down, down, down. 'Accept you as what? My lover and my boss?'

He looked deep into her eyes. 'No. I'm offering you something much more than that.'

Her heart started to race. 'What are you offering?'

'I'm offering you everything I have, everything I am. I want you at my side, Amy. For ever.'

The world was spinning around her. Fly too close to the sun, she told herself dizzily, and you won't just get your wings singed. You'll burn alive. 'Anton, I am so ordinary. You will grow tired of me very quickly. And then you'll regret those words.'

'Do you think you'll grow tired of me?' he demanded.

She could not lie to him. 'No.'

'Then you feel the same emotions that I do.'

'Anton,' she said, her voice almost breaking, 'it's easy to be infatuated with you. Every woman around you feels it. How can I really believe that you've chosen me, out of everybody?'

His expression grew sombre. 'Amy, what happened to you? What did you go through that hurt you so badly?'

'Just life.' She tried to laugh. 'Let's have a lovely day in the sun, darling man. And stop trying to get me into bed. You'd probably be so disappointed, anyway. No!' She laid her fingers on his lips to silence him. 'Don't say any more!' If she had to listen to him a moment longer, she knew her will would melt like caramel. 'Please, Anton!'

They were so close to the shore now that he had to concentrate on getting the sampan safely beached and secured with the anchor. The boat finally came to rest among the wavelets that kissed the golden shore.

They carried the picnic basket and the towels ashore and chose a place in the shade of a flowering hibiscus, whose crimson trumpets nodded over them. The meal that Anton had packed was a simple one—a freshly baked baguette, some pâté, a cooked chicken and a bottle of champagne in an icebox.

Amy accepted the glass of foaming champagne he poured for her and drank gratefully. The bread was crisp and the cold chicken was delicious. 'You are a very good provider, Captain Morgan. This is heaven!'

'And all ours.'

'Thank you for bringing me here.'

When they had finished eating, he leaned over and kissed her mouth lightly. 'Mmm, you taste of champagne.'

'Because I'm in such high spirits.'

'Oh, dear, that was a feeble pun.' He smiled at her. 'Have you noticed that there are wild bananas and mangoes growing on this island?'

'Bananas and mangoes, hmm?'

'And the rocks are full of clams. I could knock a hole in that boat and then we'd have to live here for ever.'

'On wild mangoes?'

'And each other.'

'Wouldn't we get bored?'

'I would never get bored with you.' He drew his finger softly down the line of her cheek, his fingertip brushing the delicate corner of her mouth. 'Kiss me again,' he invited softly.

'You kissed me,' she pointed out, mesmerised by his proximity.

'Then it's your turn.'

'I can't,' she pleaded. 'Even if I wanted to, I can't.'

'*Do* you want to?' he challenged.

She looked up at his mouth, that mouth she had always thought the most desirable in the world. She felt her heart turn over inside her as she lifted her mouth and kissed him. And then they were in each other's arms.

She had been kissed by other men she'd gone out with, culminating in Martin McCallum, who had been the most experienced lover she had known. But this was different. This was like no kiss had ever been. This was so serious that she felt her body melt in his strong embrace, so sublime that her spirit seemed to soar upwards with wonder.

She could only cling to him. Between kisses, he whispered her name. His mouth was hungry, tasting her eyelids, her temples, the curve of her jaw and sweet line of her throat. Amy knew that nothing in her life had ever been so intense. His body, male and hard against her, filled her with a passionate desire that made her want to devour him, her fingers almost tearing at his muscles, her teeth biting his shoulders, his neck, his lips. But far more than that, there was a spiritual dimension she had only ever encountered in her deepest dreams—the knowledge that it was Anton who was making love to her, Anton, the man she idolised above all others, the man she could never trust.

It was insane, and yet *she* was insane right now. Her erect nipples were making scandalous peaks through the flimsy fabric of her bikini top; the sight of them seemed to drive him wild, and when he began pulling her top off she helped him shamelessly, wriggling out of the garment with a husky laugh.

'God, you're so beautiful,' he whispered, lowering his dark head to claim her. Her breasts were taut, and his kiss was a torment, made so much worse when his mouth closed around her nipples, his hot tongue caressing roughly, sucking, biting.

She arched against him, her thighs parting invitingly. She could feel his arousal, hard and male against her body. She reached for him, her hands wickedly eager, and took possession. He groaned, his eyes narrowing to fierce slits.

'Are you sure this is what you want?' he asked her.

She did not answer with words, but by lifting her parted lips to his mouth.

CHAPTER ELEVEN

Now there was no need of questions or answers. She lifted her hips so he could strip off her bikini bottom, then helped him pull off his swimming trunks.

'Anton,' she murmured as he mounted her naked body, 'oh, Anton...'

The rush of the waves and the whisper of the foam made the music that accompanied their lovemaking. She was staring deep into his indigo eyes as he entered her.

She had dreamed of a wonderful lover so many times, without giving him a face or a name. But she had never met him. Until now. She had never dreamed it could be like this—so gentle, so tender, and yet so powerful. It was as though there, at the edge of the sea, she first realised what her woman's body was made for.

All the time that he made love to her, arousing her to ecstasy, he kissed her face and throat, his soft voice telling her how beautiful she was, how desirable, how wonderful. There was a profound rightness about what they were doing, she felt that in her soul. And at the moment they both reached climax tears spilled from her eyes, sliding down her cheeks to wet his face.

They were both gasping for air at the finish. He gathered her tight against his chest, whispering her name. She held on for dear life, the world still spinning around her.

'I'm sorry if I hurt you,' he said. 'Was I too rough?'

'You were perfect,' she murmured, nuzzling his chest hair blissfully. 'Just perfect.'

He caressed her body tenderly. 'You're exquisite, Amy. So beautiful. I'm the luckiest man alive.'

138

They drowsed in the shade, cradled in one another's arms. The sound of the waves lulled them, until the growing heat of midday drove them down to the water to swim.

The sea was cool and delicious. It was a flawless day, the sky without a single cloud. Amy watched in fascination as shoals of tiny multicoloured fish nibbled at her toes. The world was different now, and she was different. Her body would never be the same again. Nor would her soul. He had touched her as she had never been touched before.

Anton's strong arms closed around her, holding her close.

'I'm in heaven,' she told him.

'Why did you keep me away for so long?' he asked, kissing her neck. 'You almost drove me insane.'

'I find it very hard to trust people,' she said.

'Why shouldn't you trust me?' His dark hair was slicked back, his passionate face beaded with droplets. 'Why should you doubt me?'

'I suppose partly because I couldn't believe that you really cared about me. I still can't. And partly because I got the wrong idea about you, right from the start...in Borneo, when you kissed me, I thought you were just out to make a conquest. And then, at work...well, people said things...about Marcie...'

'That I had an affair with her?'

'Yes,' she admitted. 'And that she had to leave so suddenly because, well, she was expecting your child.'

His eyes were suddenly angry. 'Who said that?'

'I can't tell you,' she said wretchedly, 'because you'll fire the person concerned!'

'Whoever it is, he or she deserves to be fired,' he said. 'Is that what they think the clinic is all about? And you believed *that*?'

'I'm so sorry,' Amy said miserably. 'Anton, I didn't know what to believe. I was just trying to protect myself!'

He looked into her eyes. 'Amy, please tell me you don't believe that poisonous rubbish any more.'

'I believe in you,' she said simply.

He kissed her passionately. 'Come with me,' he said, 'I want to show you something.' They waded ashore, seawater cascading down their bodies. He led her up the beach and into the green shade of the trees.

'Where are we going?' she asked.

'To a special place.'

The foliage was scented with some spicy flowering plant. As he had predicted, there were wild mangoes and bananas growing on the island. The ripe fruit hung like jewels over the path. Anton pulled branches down so she could pick some of the fruit, which smelled sweet and delicious in her arms.

'We'll take some of these, too,' he said, picking fragrant white and crimson flowers from a vine. As they went on, he held her hand, guiding her over the smooth boulders, holding aside branches that occasionally blocked the way.

At the end of the path was their destination—a small, ancient pagoda that stood half-overgrown among rambutan trees.

'Oh, Anton,' she whispered, 'how lovely!'

'It's a Buddhist shrine,' he said. 'It must be hundreds of years old. It's been almost forgotten—hardly anybody remembers that it's here any more.'

They walked into the temple. The cool interior was decorated with ornate sculptures, the paintings on the walls faded but still discernible. At the back was a stone statue of the Buddha, his serene face smiling.

They stood in front of it together. The floor of the temple was littered with white sand and dried flower blossoms. The domed shape of the ancient structure seemed to capture and amplify the distant murmur of the sea. A deep peace sank into Amy's heart. This was a holy place, whatever one's religion might be.

They laid the offering of fruit and flowers at the statue's feet, then stood there, hands entwined. At that moment, Amy felt that nothing could ever touch their happiness. It was as though they had undergone some sacred ceremony that had bound them together for ever, protecting them from all harm.

'Thank you for bringing me here,' she whispered. 'I'll never forget it.'

They walked back in silence. In the shade of their hibiscus grove, they lay down in one another's arms again.

'Today, our lives start afresh,' he whispered.

'Yes,' she said quietly.

'You've made me so happy today, Amy. I've wanted you ever since you walked into my life, that morning at Kai Tak. I think I felt it even before I saw you, because I should have left for Borneo the day before. But something kept me there, waiting for you. Something told me that I had to meet you. And from the moment I saw your face, I loved you. I didn't think it would happen like this—spontaneously, on a beach in Vietnam. In fact, I didn't really know how it would happen. But I always knew that we would be lovers, and belong to each other completely.'

She looked into the depths of his eyes. 'Anton, forgive me for not trusting you. Things have happened to me that hurt me badly—and—and made it hard for me to give myself. But I have loved you for such a long time!'

His warm fingers cupped her chin and lifted her face so he could kiss her soft mouth. 'My golden girl,' he whispered, 'whatever has hurt you, I will take it away.'

Her eyes closed languidly as he kissed her lips. His mouth was like velvet, so tender and yet so commanding. His arms were so strong as they drew her close to him. No man had ever affected her like this. No man ever would. She whimpered, clinging to his powerful shoulders as their kiss deepened into searing passion. It was as though everything else in the world had disappeared, and nothing was real any more except their two beating hearts.

Kissing her sweetly on the eyelids and mouth, he was slow and gentle this time. He was in complete, masterful control. The muscles rippled unhurriedly beneath his tanned skin. He looked down at her. His eyes seemed to darken with hunger. 'You are so beautiful,' he whispered. 'Your breasts, the swell of your hips…so perfect. I've never touched anything as fine as your skin.'

She shuddered, her back arching, as he caressed her, lovingly, expertly. When he kissed her lips again, her mouth opened under the pressure of his tongue. The maelstrom of passion that she knew so well was sucking her down. She clung to his neck as though she had found herself in a real whirlpool, as though there were real danger that she might be engulfed for ever.

When his fingers found the tender moistness between her thighs, they brought a pleasure that made her senses swim.

He slid down, his mouth seeking her. An attempt at modesty made her try to resist, but her own body betrayed her. Her thighs parted to open herself to him, and her hips rose so that he could claim her secret places with his mouth.

His kiss was gentle at first. But she heard him moan with satisfaction as he tasted her, his tongue sinful and hungry. Amy gasped with pleasure, then could not stop herself from moaning aloud as his strong arms slipped around her hips and pulled her to him.

Over the years she had wondered why it was she could find no man who could unlock her secrets, not even Martin; she had wondered whether she was cold, unresponsive. Unresponsive! The way her body and soul felt right now, she knew that she was every inch a woman. It had simply taken the right man to open up her feelings.

Anton's mouth was hungry and hot, and he seemed to want to devour her, just as much as she ached to be devoured. How heavenly it was to be consumed like this, to be wanted like this! Her fingers threaded through his crisp, dark hair, her heels caressing the strong muscles of his back. Pleasure peaked so intensely that she could not stop herself from sliding dizzily over the edge...and then she was in a world where she had never been, a world where music and colour and passion exploded into one overpowering emotion that was so great, the tears spontaneously flooded her eyes.

He held her until her shuddering faded into stillness, his mouth coaxing every last drop of pleasure from her body.

'Anton,' she whispered. 'Please come to me...'

He obeyed her, gathering her slim body in his muscular arms, holding her so tight that she whimpered with pleasure. He murmured her name softly, tenderly, but spoke no other words. Locked in the passion of their embrace, Amy caressed his body, feeling the power of his man's strength, yet aware of how sensitive his shuddering responses were.

His arousal was as rampant as it had been that morning. She caressed him gently with her fingertips. The velvety skin of his sex was hot, and his arching pleasure thrilled her. He kissed her with fierce passion, his hands cupping her hips, his desire pressing urgently between her thighs.

Amy rolled back and pulled him onto her. Her eyes searched his face intently, searching for the emotion in his eyes.

'You are mine,' he said, as though answering her unspoken question, 'mine, mine. Only mine.'

He entered her body, but far more carefully than he had done the first time. This time he was slow, unhurried, allowing them both to savour the way their bodies united, his sliding deep into her, hers stretching to accommodate him.

When he was fully inside her, he kissed her eyelids and then her mouth. 'I have never felt anything like this,' he told her softly. He was cradling her shoulders in his arms, the dominant weight of his hips pressing hers back against the sand. 'I'll never let you go, Amy.'

Those words were exactly what she wanted to hear. He made love to her with exquisite tenderness and skill, controlling her responses, exciting her, until the pleasure was deep and overwhelmingly delicious. She whimpered his name, her mouth open against his, their kisses growing more abandoned as their lovemaking intensified.

Anton's ragged breathing told her he was as ready as she was. She knew that they were going to the same place together, soon, very soon...

This time her climax was different, a searing sunburst that melted her body and dazzled her mind. Anton crushed her to him, his shuddering in perfect time with hers. Gasping, they clung to one another, their limbs twining until peace descended on them.

He smiled down at her, caressing her breasts and stomach tenderly.

'You're so beautiful,' he told her. 'I want to drink you in with my soul. You are the centre of my universe. You are all I will ever want.'

Amy would always remember that day as the most beautiful of her life. And the remainder of their stay in Vietnam, too, was like a wonderful dream. The lovely villa with the lily pond became their palace, their world. Warm, scented days blended into dark, thrilling nights.

When work called, and they travelled back to Vung Tao for consultations with the engineers, she was at his side, unable to take her eyes off him, this magnificent man who had chosen her, whose every waking thought seemed only to be to please her and fill her with delight. She was so proud of him, of the care he took of his world. She was living in paradise.

Though she was aware that paradise was only leased, that they would soon have to return to Hong Kong and the complexities of their future there, she gave herself up utterly to the moment, and to Anton, as though both were for ever.

They wandered around the charming city of Saigon together, visiting museums and temples, dreamily watching the fleets of bicycles or the groups of people, old and young, performing the stately callisthenics of t'ai chi in the public squares, under flowering trees.

They sat on the tranquil banks of the River Saigon, watching the endless and multifarious flow of traffic, from huge rice barges to tiny little skiffs, threading their way through one another's wakes; and talked endlessly, as lovers did.

They dined at food stalls in the markets and in fancy restaurants. One memorable evening, he took her to the Ben Thanh Restaurant, one of the most famous in Asia, where they had the classic Vietnamese dish, *cha gio*, made from minced crab meat, pork, fragrant mushrooms and bean sprouts, wrapped in a thin rice pancake and then deep fried. The crisp little rolls were utterly delicious, eaten wrapped in a lettuce leaf and dipped in a variety of savoury sauces.

And then, their last night in Saigon was upon them.

'I can't believe we have to go back tomorrow,' she whispered as they lay in bed together.

'What difference will it make?' he asked.

'Things will change.'

'They won't, my darling.'

But she had a dark foreboding. 'You have to be in London soon for the chairman's report. Lavinia will be waiting. You'll start to realise that even though you like me, she has so much more to offer. You'll spend hours with her, just like in France and—'

'Amy!'

'People will be talking about me. The way they did about

Marcie. They'll be laughing behind my back, saying things—'

'Hey.' His caressing hand had been tracing erotic circles on her belly, moving ever lower to the dangerous regions where her reactions were starting to quiver hotly. 'What's got into you, my golden girl? I've never heard you talk like this!'

'Oh, Anton, I'm so afraid!'

'Afraid of what?' he asked softly. His fingers expertly teased her, slipping liquidly across her most sensitive places until delicious pleasure swelled and grew between her thighs.

He seemed to know her every secret. There was no button he did not know how to push, no pleasure he did not completely understand. She had learned more about her body this week than in the previous twenty years. Anton understood her far, far better than she understood herself.

She could only cling to him as he brought her back into that enchanted kingdom of sensual delight, and then led her with utter assurance to another exquisite climax.

Partly because she could not help it, she sank her teeth into his shoulder as he prolonged her pleasure, almost past the point she could bear. She quivered and whimpered, and finally came to rest with her head on his broad chest, his hands gentling her.

'What are you doing to me?' she panted.

'Don't I make you happy?'

'You take me to places I've never been in my life.'

'You do the same to me.'

'But you must have been with so many women. You're so experienced, and I feel so clumsy.'

'You are never clumsy,' he said, crushing her in his arms. 'You are my one true love.'

Amy awoke in the early dawn. There was a rosy tinge to the sky. She was cradled securely in the arms of her lover

He held her possessively, assuredly, even in sleep. She could hear his even breathing, feel his warm breath on her neck. Her skin smelled of their lovemaking. Her body had never felt like this before. Anton had made love to her so passionately, in so many ways, that it was as though he had dismantled her and then put her together again in a new shape.

She thought about their lovemaking with something bordering on disbelief. She'd had no idea that sex could be anything like this.

Sex. The word seemed so inadequate to cover what he had shown her this week. It was far more than the physical coupling she had always understood by the word. What he had done to her was show her what lay within her own soul. She was changed by it, altered for ever.

It had been a kind of divine madness, a hurricane that had swept through her life without warning. But where would it take her?

An ominous sinking in the pit of her stomach reminded her that within a few hours they had to fly back to Hong Kong.

She was suddenly afraid, very afraid. Her terrified mind was telling her that she was in desperate danger of seeing her dreams crash and burn. It was telling her to run as fast as she could, to fly for her life, before Anton destroyed her heart.

She tried to recapture the deep peace that had filled her in the pagoda on their island. But it eluded her obstinately. There was only anxiety.

Her tension must have wakened Anton. He kissed her face and throat softly, cupping her breasts with his palms. 'Don't worry,' he whispered, as though he had sensed her terror in his sleep, 'everything's going to be all right.'

There was no need of words between them. He made love

to her tenderly, their unhurried movements in complete harmony, until ecstasy and then peace settled around them.

She fell back asleep almost at once, her head cradled in his arms, her cheek pressed against his chest so that she could hear nothing but the deep, steady beat of his heart.

CHAPTER TWELVE

'Do you like it?'

They had walked out onto the terrace of the house. Hong Kong was spread out below them. Anton was looking at her enquiringly.

'It's stunning,' she said. 'You're not seriously thinking of buying it?'

'I've always had my eye on it. It seemed providential when it came up for sale.'

'Well, it's the loveliest house I've seen. But you don't need anything this big!'

The property, called Quilin House, was high on Victoria Peak. With enamelled dragons and other mythical beasts curvetting at the ends of the roof-beams, it was an airy, six-bedroom palace, with a vast balcony commanding a wonderful view of the harbour. It boasted a luxurious pool and parking for five cars in the basement. And it had a stunning natural setting. From the carefully tended garden you could walk straight into forests of bamboo, fern and wild hibiscus on the peak. As they stood on the balcony they were watching kites and hawks gliding on the thermals two thousand feet above the harbour.

She didn't even want to know what they were asking for this property. In Hong Kong, the most cramped apartments commanded a premium.

'Why do you think it's too big?' he asked, looking at her.

She smiled at him. 'Six bedrooms? There's only one of you, remember?'

He put his arm round her waist and drew her close. 'There

are two of us. And what if we have a dozen children?' he murmured into her ear. 'Then it will be too small!'

She kissed him, her heart fluttering. 'I haven't agreed to have *any* children, my lord and master. And you haven't asked me if I want to move in with you!'

'I'm asking you now.'

'You are a crazy man. Why are there dragons on the roof-beams?'

'It's *feng shui*. They guard all four quarters of the house from harm.'

The real-estate agent came out, unfolding her brochure. 'Quilin House has a long history, Mr and Mrs Zell,' she said, beaming. 'The property is unique. As you both know, luxury like this is rare in our city. It's a once-in-a-lifetime opportunity.'

'What was the price?' Anton asked, watching the hawks wheel and glide.

Without batting an eyelid, the realtor named a figure in the high millions.

'Will they take half a million less?'

'They might do,' the realtor said, her eyes gleaming.

'Very good,' Anton said, holding Amy's hand and facing her. 'We'll get a written offer to you in an hour or so. We'll be in London from tomorrow, so I would like an answer today, if possible. I'll give you my number. You can contact me any time. I'll be waiting.'

Amy turned away. She was suddenly remembering something Gerda had said to her in France:

I see now! You think that once they are married, he will install you as his mistress in some lacquered palace in Hong Kong!

At the time, the words had seemed more like a gratuitous insult than a real insight. But perhaps Gerda Meyer was a woman of the world, after all. Perhaps she understood things better than Amy ever could.

Was this not exactly the 'lacquered palace' Gerda had predicted? The most beautiful house in Hong Kong—but in reality nothing more than a golden cage for a kept bird?

After all, he was talking about living together, having children together—but he had not mentioned marriage.

A business wife in France and a pleasure wife in Hong Kong? Oh, yes, he is man enough for that.

And I know men like Anton Zell. They want it all—and they always get to have it all.

Empresses sometimes tolerate a concubine—or two.

Suddenly the magnificent house seemed like a prison to her, a place where all her hopes and joys would slowly die.

In Borneo he had told her clearly that he could never marry, that he had no space or time for women—'the sort of women who want a commitment from a man'. He had told her he was married to his work.

Perhaps he had meant that more literally than she had understood at the time. If he married Lavinia, he really *would* be marrying his work.

As they drove down from the peak, Amy's heart was as heavy as lead. 'I didn't think you were serious until the last minute. Are you really planning that house for—?'

'For us,' he finished. 'Yes.'

'What kind of "us"?'

'You and me. Living together. Don't you like the house?'

'It's your money, Anton,' she said, 'there's nothing for me to like or dislike!'

'Amy, I want us to have a life together from now on. Can't you see that? Don't you understand the way I feel about you? Don't you see how vital you are to me—emotionally, at work, in every way?'

Her heart was beating like a trapped bird against a window pane. Since Vietnam, everything had moved so fast. The pace of work had been hectic—this time, not the practical slog of travelling and touring plants, but the endless paperwork involved in preparing for the corporation's annual general meeting, at which Anton was due to deliver his annual report to a potentially stormy quorum of stockholders.

The report itself, of course, had already been printed—much of the work having fallen to Amy—and mailed to the stockholders. Anton had entrusted Amy with supervising the 'corporate identity' of the report. She had decided that a new look was necessary to communicate the dynamic new direction the corporation was taking. She had worked closely with a cutting-edge team of three graphic designers to produce a seventy-five-page, glossy illustrated report that outlined the global expansion envisaged by Anton while emphasising the solid base of past success from which they were working.

She herself had worked up the tagline 'New Technology, New World', and had redesigned the Zell logo as a blue globe with the green letter Z moulding itself to the sphere. It spoke plainly of Zell Corporation's commitment to ecology and the dominant role it intended to play in recycling technology from now on.

However, taking her cue from Lavinia Carron, she had avoided using *recycling*, 'the least stylish word in the English language', overmuch, and had substituted phrases like *resource renewal*, instead. But the message was clear—Anton intended to take the company ever further into the field of reprocessing that he had opened up with his new technology.

Anton—and everybody else—had been very impressed by the result. The new corporate emblem was going to be adopted and would soon be mounted on the blue tower block. The report was going to be convincing to everyone except the hard-core dissenters.

Anton had already been interviewed by regulars from both the *Economist* and the *Financial Times*, and the forthcoming articles looked set to bring favourable publicity to the new direction.

In the spaces left by this concentrated work, their private life had been even more intense. Like lava flowing at white heat through the veins in rock, it had followed its own course where it could. When the pressure of work gave them a little space alone together, there had been no words; just a fierce desire that incandesced in a moment. Tearing off each other's clothes, making love with frantic passion, falling into an exhausted sleep in one another's arms, waking just in time to wash, dress and rush back to work—that had been the tenor of their days.

Those golden hours on the island, those long evenings in Saigon, were like a distant dream. Though in Vietnam Anton had spoken of getting his priorities right, back in Hong Kong they had been thrown into a maelstrom of activity that left no time to say what needed to be said, or reflect on what needed to be contemplated.

She had never known passion as intense as this, had never known that her body could blaze like a star at a man's slightest touch; but there had also been something terrifying about the speed at which everything was happening. She was beginning to feel like someone driving a very fast car— and the faster the car went, the more the acceleration pushed her against the seat, the less in control she felt.

And now, a few hours before they were due to fly to London, he had rushed her up the peak to look at that palatial house and was talking about buying it for them to live in together.

But not about marriage.

'Anton,' she said in a quiet voice, 'shouldn't we wait until we get back from London before we start taking all these decisions?'

'You know what the property market is like in Hong Kong, darling,' he said. 'If we wait more than a few hours, that house will be sold. Quilin House is one of the most famous properties in the city.'

'There will be other houses. And it's so much money. I know that money isn't much of an object with a zillionaire like you, but you're making an offer of many millions on a house before we've even worked out what we both want.'

'There has been so little time since we got back from Saigon,' he said, the powerful engine of the car throbbing as it snarled impatiently in the traffic.

'That's exactly what I mean,' she replied, looking at him. 'We have no time to talk. No time to plan, let alone just be together!'

He met her eyes with that dazzling smile. 'Do you love me?'

'Yes,' she sighed, 'I love you insanely.'

'And I adore you,' he replied. 'What else is there to talk about?'

'We need to know that what we're doing is really what we want. You're the archetypal bachelor millionaire and I am the latest addition to the company. You know what people will say about us—what they're already saying!'

'What are they saying?' he asked, accelerating through a gap in the traffic jam.

'That I'm your latest—concubine.'

'Do *you* think you're a concubine?'

'I don't know what I am,' she said with painful honesty. 'We know so little about each other.'

'I know all that matters about you. Unless you've kept a dark secret from me?'

'Dear man, I have secrets that I even keep from myself,' she retorted with a wry smile. 'I keep telling you, I may look like an angel, but appearances can be deceptive!'

'I don't think you could deceive me,' he said. 'As for the things my staff might be saying about me, I really don' care. The next person to spread poisonous gossip about me might find him or herself unemployed.'

It was only with difficulty that she had persuaded him not to fire Glynnis, the medical officer who had put two and two together to make five.

'And what about the things Lavinia Carron might be saying about you?' she asked. 'If she gets an inkling that you and I are lovers, she could turn very nasty. And she will be waiting for you in London…darling boy.'

'It has nothing to do with her. Do you really think that I'm so afraid of Lavinia?'

'I don't think you're afraid of anything,' Amy said. 'That's the problem. Your company *is* you, Anton. It comes down to one man, to a much greater extent than with any other company of this size that I know of. It relies on your genius, your ideas, your character. But that also makes you potentially vulnerable. If Lavinia mounts a personal attack on you, you could lose the reins.'

'I can handle Lavinia.'

'You can handle her while she thinks you're going to marry her.'

She waited for him to say something, her heart pounding in her throat. Would he deny it? Would he admit that marrying Lavinia was part of his plan? That installing Amy as his mistress in Quilin House was the other half?

'I don't intend to let Lavinia dictate the company's future,' he said at last.

'Then how will you stop her? She only needs to get a few others on her side. She'll say that you're losing your touch. Making misjudgements that will cost the stockholders money. She'll point to the risks you're taking with the new plants, to your sale of the Marseilles refinery to Henri Barbusse, to your plans in south-east Asia. At the AGM, she'll say those are all bad miscalculations. And in private, she'll tell everybody you've lost your head over an impertinent little nobody—me—who supports you in your wild ventures.'

'But you do support me in my wild ventures. And I adore you for it!'

'You have so much to lose, Anton. The last thing you should be doing is advertising me. And I can't bear the idea of becoming a weapon that unscrupulous people might use to harm you in any way!'

'So I should keep you in the background?' he smiled.

'That's what *taipans* have always done with their girl-friends,' she said, echoing what Gerda had said. 'I'm perfectly happy in Causeway Bay, you have the Wanchai apartment. Living together and buying a huge house is premature. Let's leave it until we're more certain.'

The glance he gave her contained a glitter of anger. 'I've never done this before, Amy,' he said in a quiet voice. 'I never committed myself to any woman, never made promises, never said those words, *I love you.*'

'Anton—'

'I waited half my life for the right woman. And now that you're here, and I am committing myself and all that I am to you, you tell me that you're not certain.'

'I don't know how you can be certain, either!' she exclaimed. 'We love each other madly, and when we make love the world stops turning. But you know as well as I do that relationships are built on more than that!'

'Well, what *are* relationships built on?' he demanded. 'What was your last relationship built on, Amy?'

She fell silent. It had been built on lies and exploitation, but she could not tell him that.

'You haven't even told me his name,' he went on harshly. 'You won't talk about what happened. But I get the feeling that I am being penalised now for whatever it was *he* did to you!'

Again, she had no answer. Perhaps because much of wha

he said was true. She *was* penalising Anton for what Martin had done to her. But her very inability to tell Anton what had happened to her made her afraid that everything was moving too fast. She wasn't ready. Like a wounded doe, she needed time and patience before she could come out of the thorny thicket where she had buried herself so deeply. If only Anton could see that!

And if only he could understand that her needing time did not mean she didn't love him! On the contrary, she adored him with every fibre of her being. Nor did she doubt that he loved her just as passionately. But did she love him so madly that she was prepared to become his mistress—and perhaps have his children—and have to watch him marry Lavinia...and know she would never be his wife?

Their jet took off at five in the afternoon. As it rose swiftly over the city, Amy saw the Zell Corporation tower flit under their wings. But in the sunset, the blue windows were now blood-red.

She thought about her arrival in this city, the first time she had seen that glass tower. It had only been a few short months earlier, yet a whole lifetime had been compressed into that time. So much had happened to her; she was hardly the same woman who had been on that other flight.

It was typical of their lives at this moment that the only quiet time they had together was on an airplane. And even here, Anton was brooding over his laptop, assimilating the latest information as it came in, so that he could give his stockholders the latest news.

She curled up on the seat next to him—once again, there were only two of them in the spacious cabin—and passed him the whisky and cola that had become their sundown ritual, the crystal tumbler to be shared by both of them.

'Are you ready to face the stockholders?' she asked.

'Dividends are higher this quarter than ever before,' he commented. 'They ought to roll out the red carpet for me.'

'Or the guillotine.' As in commercial airliners, soothing jazz was drifting out of the speakers, designed to allay the terrors of take-off. She snuggled up to him and rested her golden head on his shoulder.

'Tired?' he asked.

'It's been a long day.'

Anton pushed the table aside, shutting his laptop. He pulled a blanket over them both, put his arm around her and drew her close.

'I contacted the real-estate agent and told her we wouldn't be putting in an offer until next week,' he told her.

'I'm sorry,' she murmured. 'I know how you wanted to buy that house for us.'

'It may still be there when we get back. But as you said, there will always be other houses.'

'I love you so much,' she said, stroking his face. 'I hate you to be disappointed in me. But we have nothing to lose by taking things slow.'

'And what do we have to lose by taking things fast?' he asked with a smile that she could feel with her fingertips.

'You might regret having committed so much to me,' she replied. 'You might want your heart back.'

'And will you give it to me?'

'I will give you anything you want.'

The Lear jet was soaring up into a clear sky that darkened from violet into ultramarine. Below them, in a glittering, twilit sea, islands were scattered like jewels. The smoky music of the saxophones was peaceful.

Under the warmth of the blanket, his hand caressed her stomach. 'I only want you. The rest of it can go hang.'

'You've got me. But I'm afraid of the trouble I may cause you.'

Anton kissed her lips tenderly. His kisses were always so

erotic; no man had ever kissed her in this way, not taking, but giving, a velvety caress that was so sweet. She felt his hand slide under the waistband of her pants and move downwards.

'You've lost weight,' he accused.

'I'm just sucking in my tummy,' she whispered.

He kissed her lips again, then her eyelids. 'Don't worry about anything. We were meant to be together. And as soon as you let me, I'm going to buy you a beautiful big house where we can lock the doors, draw the curtains, turn out the lights and...'

His hand had slipped into her panties now. His fingertips caressed her soft curls, sliding between her thighs to where she was already wet and waiting for him. He cupped the warm mound of her sex in his possessive palm.

'And?' she asked, her breath catching in her throat.

'And do this.' The touch of his fingers on her sex was, as always, shockingly intense, bursting on her senses the way a honey-sweet grape burst in the mouth.

One of the things she most loved about Anton was the way he knew how to touch her, any place, any time, in any number of ways, and fill her soul with delight. His caress was rhythmical, expert, making her response grow and swell like a tropical wave.

She reached her own hand between his legs and found his arousal, thrusting passionately towards her. Panting with desire now, she explored, finding the way in through zips and pleats until she could wrap her fingers around him. He was hot and thick and long, and she wanted him desperately inside her.

Kissing hungrily, their mouths locked together, they manoeuvred in the wide seats until she got him exactly where she wanted him—pressing on top of her, his manhood thrusting between her yielding thighs.

It was so delicious, so fulfilling, to feel him slide into her body, stretching her, filling her, taking the love deep into her soul. Their lovemaking was slow and exquisitely prolonged, each searching for every corner of pleasure in the other, each wanting to give every possible ounce of fulfilment; until, with a rush like an ocean wave, their climax swept them both up into heaven.

She lay satiated, drugged with his love, her head cradled on his chest. Out of the window, she could see a velvety sky spattered with diamond stars. At these moments, there were no doubts for her. She was alive and on this planet only to be with Anton. Nothing else mattered, or ever would.

That was the power of sex. It was anti-thought, anti-caution. No doubt Mother Nature had planned it that way to ensure the continuation of the species, no matter what obliteration threatened!

CHAPTER THIRTEEN

IT WAS a long flight. Through the dark, star-spangled night they made love again, slept, then made love yet again. It was, Amy thought, by far the best way anyone had yet discovered to pass an intercontinental flight. She wished that they might never have to land back on earth again.

But the red glow of dawn appeared at last and coming back to earth could no longer be postponed. Britain appeared in the distance as a dark and rumpled mass of cloud that looked like a huge counterpane.

As they descended through the cloud layer, however, the illusion of softness was soon dispelled. It was December weather in northern Europe. Darkness closed in, lit only by lurid flares of lightning. Turbulence shook the Lear as strong winds battered the jet. Amy watched apprehensively as heavy ice formed swiftly at the windows. It became perceptibly very much colder. When the Lear finally descended from the maelstrom it was to find itself above a city lashed by a snowstorm, bathed in a dim and unearthly grey light.

'Well,' Anton said, hugging Amy, 'time to face the music. Buckle up!'

The landing at Heathrow was made in driving snow and violent cross-winds that made the Lear stagger and seem to stall in the air. Amy clutched Anton's strong arm for comfort as they bounced down the runway. Why was it that so many of their moments together had been marked by storms and rain?

The reality of London was dark, bitterly cold and very snowy. In the taxi to the Ritz, where they were going to be staying, Amy switched on the satellite phone and at once the calls began to pour in. With every passing minute, the intimate warmth that had been built up so deliciously between them during the night flight was giving way to the endless clamour of work.

The great hotel, however, with its atmosphere of a French château somehow magically dropped in the middle of Piccadilly, was a welcoming monolith. With its Christmas lights and cheerily illuminated windows, it resembled an ocean liner looming out of the whirling flakes of snow.

Their suite was breathtaking, bearing witness to the refurbishment that had restored every tassel, every gleaming piece of furniture and every crystal in the chandeliers to their original Louis XVI style. Watching the snowflakes whirl against the windows from within the glowing luxury of a room like this was delicious.

Amy half expected to see King Louis himself—or at least Napoleon—reclining on the ornate four-poster bed. But it was wonderfully empty and she sprawled on it happily with the newspapers that had been thoughtfully provided.

At huge expense, Anton had booked the famous Marie Antoinette Suite here at the Ritz for tonight's reception. The glorious room, one of the most famous venues in London, would make an opulent setting for Anton to entertain the several dozen major stockholders in advance of tomorrow's AGM, which would be held at a modern conference room overlooking the Thames.

While Anton talked on the phone, she opened the *Financial Times*, expecting to find an article in advance of tomorrow's stockholders' meeting. It was there, all right, but its tone made her sit up, frowning.

'You'd better read this, darling,' she said.

Anton read the article carefully, starting with the headline, NEW DIRECTION FOR ZELL CORPORATION QUESTIONED BY SHAREHOLDERS.

When he'd finished, he passed the newspaper back to her.

'It doesn't say who any of these supposed shareholders are. I don't take that too seriously.'

'Well, it's obvious who one of them is,' Amy said. 'Though, as you say, it doesn't quote her name.'

'You can't blame everything on Lavinia, darling,' Anton said with a smile. 'It's just a journalist picking up a possible story, that's all. They'll be singing a different song after the AGM.' He glanced at his watch. He was scheduled to meet Lavinia Carron for drinks before lunch. Ostensibly, she was welcoming an old friend to London, but Amy feared it would be the first clash of sabres between them. 'I'm guessing you have no desire to rekindle the flames of friendship with Lavinia?'

'I never want to see her again,' Amy said. 'I'm sure she's behind that story, my darling. It's a shot across your bows.'

He came to sit beside her, took her face in both his hands, and kissed her carefully on the mouth. 'Don't worry about a thing.'

'I can't help worrying,' she replied, searching his eyes with her own. 'She wants your money or to be your wife, Anton!'

He laughed. 'Sit tight, angel. What are you going to do while I hobnob with Lavinia?'

'I'll do some shopping.'

'OK, we'll meet for lunch at the Savoy Grill—I feel like something quintessentially English. One o'clock, Miss Worthington. Don't be late!'

She had told Anton that she was going shopping but the truth was there was almost nothing she needed. Her life in Hong Kong was so pampered and the shopping there was more than adequate for her relatively undemanding tastes. Of clothes, cosmetics and accessories, she already had more than she could use.

And the sinking feeling that persisted in the pit of her

stomach would not have allowed herself to spend on luxuries, anyway.

Books, however, were another matter. The prospect of losing herself in a sea of the latest books was very alluring indeed. Belting herself into a coat, she headed purposefully out to tour the large book emporiums of the city.

It was very cold. As so often, London seemed to have been taken by surprise by heavy snow. It was piled in dirty mounds, uncollected, on the traffic islands and pavements, or spread in slushy marshes that the traffic sprayed on hapless pedestrians. It was also, however, very beautiful; the great parks were stark snowfields where nobody had yet ventured to leave footprints, and each famous building, monument or statue was decorated with white caps on any horizontal plane where the stuff could adhere.

Amy roamed the bookstores, buying things for Anton as well as for herself. Exciting new books were about the only Christmas present she knew he would enjoy. Heaven knew when they would have time to read all the volumes that soon accumulated in piles on the counters, but she could always dream of a peaceful future where she and Anton would have time to please themselves and nobody else.

She tried not to think of what might be passing between Anton and Lavinia as she paged through the glossy books that still smelled of new paper and fresh ink. For all his light-hearted assurances, she was aware that the next few days were going to prove a watershed for Anton. She was not so prone to melodrama as to cast it as a battle for one man's soul—but one of the reasons she had persuaded Anton not to make an offer on Quilin House was that deep down inside, she knew that there was going to be a winner and a loser. And she knew she was going to be the loser.

Because she knew that love did not conquer all. Love was conquered by many things—by money, by expedience, by power. And Lavinia had them all on her side.

All she herself had was the miracle that Anton had fallen in love with her—one snowflake out of so many others. One snowflake that would melt as soon as it was touched by the breath of reality.

She bought so many books that there was no way she could carry them all, so they were sent to their suite at the Ritz. And then it was time for her to hurry across to the Strand to meet Anton at the Savoy.

The front of the hotel was crowded as always with Rolls-Royces and limousines trying to get their occupants as close to the entrance as possible. A uniformed commissionaire hurried out to her cab and ushered her in under the shelter of a large black umbrella.

The restaurant was crowded but she saw Anton at once, sitting at a banquette alone, his chin resting on his clasped hands. Her heart sank at his pose—she could tell at once that something was wrong. The drinks with Lavinia had evidently not gone well.

A waiter ushered her to the table and she settled down opposite Anton, trying to smile brightly. 'Sorry I'm late—the traffic's awful.'

Anton looked up at her. For the first time since she had known him, his eyes seemed empty and cold. That, more than anything, chilled her to the bone. She reached out for his hands.

'Darling, what's the matter? Did the meeting go badly?'

He pulled his hands away from hers. 'Why didn't you tell me?' he asked in a quiet voice.

'Tell you what?' she replied in shock.

'Why did I have to hear about that from Lavinia Carron, Amy?' His face, always so handsome and alive, looked like a mask of anger and pain. 'Couldn't you have told me before?'

'I don't understand what you're talking about,' she replied urgently. 'Whatever Lavinia has said to upset you so much is a lie, I can promise you that!'

'I don't think so,' he said flatly. 'I think it's you who have lied to me.'

'I have never lied to you,' she flashed back at him.

The waiter, who had been hovering with the menus, discreetly vanished at this point, though they barely noticed. The elegant restaurant, with its light wood panelling and snowy linen surmounted by bunches of pale yellow roses, seemed to be spinning around Amy.

'When you first came to me,' Anton said grimly, 'I asked you directly whether you had had an affair with Martin McCallum.'

'Oh,' she said, realisation hitting her like an arrow thudding into her heart, the shock spreading through her body, paralysing her.

'You flatly denied it,' Anton went on. 'I asked you if that was why you were so eager to leave McCallum and Roe. You denied that, too.'

'Anton, those questions weren't ethical at that point, and you know that. You had no right to ask them.'

'But you chose to answer them,' he pointed out with ineluctable logic. 'You answered them with lies.'

'Yes,' she said hopelessly, 'I lied to you.'

'We became lovers, Amy. You've had months to tell me the truth. To correct those lies. But you never did.'

'I warned you,' she said quietly. 'There are things about me that I hide even from myself. I'm not an angel. I'm very sorry that Lavinia was the one to tell you. I should have guessed she would make enquiries about me and find that out. Of course she would use it.'

'She didn't have to look very far, Amy. McCallum and Roe are one of the companies she owns shares in. A lot of shares. Of course the boy would take her into his confidence.'

'Of course he would,' she said drily. 'I have been a fool.'

Anton's eyes never left hers. 'I've been the fool, Amy. I allowed myself to believe things about you that I haven't believed of any other human being—that you were honest, that you were pure, that you were different from all the others.'

'Those are the things I believed about you, too,' she said dully.

'I even persuaded myself that we were the same inside,' he went on. 'We'd come from the same pain, we'd travelled the same route. I thought we believed in the same things, about people, about the world.'

'And don't we?'

'I don't think so, Amy. I could never lie to you the way you have lied to me. I asked you those questions during the interview because I was afraid that you'd had an affair with your last employer. You lied to me.'

'And yet, within hours of taking me on, you were telling me you wanted a "special relationship" with me, Anton,' she shot back. 'You kissed me on the lips in Borneo.'

'I did not expect or plan to fall in love with you!'

'Nor did I expect or plan to fall in love with *you*, Anton. Don't you remember how I tried to avoid it? Have you forgotten how angry you used to get with me when I wouldn't just jump into your bed?'

'Why didn't you tell me the truth?'

'For what it's worth, I always planned to tell you about Martin. I knew that there were things in my past that might upset you. That was why I was trying to put the brakes on— until I could get the chance to talk about them.'

'Somehow that chance never came.'

'Don't sound so bitter,' she begged. 'It never came because our life together is so hectic. People in love need time and space to learn about each other. You cannot find the truth about someone just through sleeping with them. If there isn't ever a moment to relax together, how can there be communication?'

'I see. So the fault is mine.'

'The fault is mine,' she replied. 'I'm just trying to tell you why I never got around to telling you about Martin. The only time we have ever had together that we weren't travelling at the speed of light was in Vietnam. And that time—' Tears filled her eyes suddenly and she could not speak for a moment. 'And that time,' she went on, brushing the wetness off her cheeks with shaking hands, 'was so precious and beautiful. I didn't want to even think about my life before you. I couldn't bear to bring up such ugly things.'

'I wish you had. It might have made a difference.'

'I'm sorry, Anton,' she repeated. 'Yes, I had an affair with Martin McCallum and I wish it had never happened.'

'It's much more than that,' he said, his eyes darkening. 'You're still hiding the truth. The truth is that you got pregnant. Didn't you?'

The room was spinning faster and faster now, the yellow roses blurring into the panelling, the elegant light fittings dazzling her aching eyes. 'Anton—'

'You got pregnant and you used that to try and force Martin McCallum into marrying you. And when that didn't work, you terminated the pregnancy. As callously and as cynically as that. And you tell me not to be bitter?'

'Anton, I can't stay here,' she heard herself say. 'I have to go.'

She rose. A deadly wave of dizziness rushed into her brain. She had to clutch the table to stop herself from falling.

Anton had risen, too. He faced her across the table, his mouth compressed into a hard line, his normally tanned face pale with emotion. 'Haven't you got anything to say?' he demanded.

Conversation around them had halted and people at neighbouring tables were staring curiously. She was aware of everything through a spiralling haze. She knew only that she had to get out of Anton's presence before she fainted or was sick all over the Savoy's snowy white linen.

'No,' she whispered. 'I haven't got anything to say, Anton.'

She clutched her bag and stumbled out of the restaurant. The alert waiter was waiting with her coat. 'Can I get the commissionaire to call you a cab, miss?' he asked her in concern.

Not trusting herself to speak, she just shook her head. She made her way frantically through the noisy crowds in the lobby.

And then she was running blindly into the whirling snow.

She found herself back in Piccadilly, at Green Park. She was not sure how she had got there. The vast white space of the park drew her in, though she was already icy cold and shivering.

Snow banks were piled high. The paths had been shovelled at some point but the heavy snowfalls had all but obliterated them again. The snow had also mocked the bare trees by piling every branch and twig with a glittering foliage of ice crystals.

Amy walked through the park, finding a wilderness in the heart of the bustling city. Soon, the loudest sound in the world was the beating of her own heart. The only life was the clouding of her breath in the icy air. Flurries of snow twirled and fluttered down constantly.

Her mind was largely a blank. She wasn't rehearsing what she might say to Anton when he finally returned to her— there was nothing to rehearse. There was only the truth. And the truth would come out of her in its own way, whether she tried to put it into clever words or not, no matter how she tried to phrase it.

She saw nobody in the park. Her frantic heartbeat began

to slow as the icy cold sank into her flesh and bone. Shuddering now with the severe drop in temperature as the afternoon closed in and it grew dark, she turned her steps back towards the Ritz.

The sparkling façade of the great hotel was like a beacon in the gloom, the famous name spelled out in lights. It was like another world, a glittering ocean liner from which she had fallen into deep, dark waters.

As she walked into the lobby she mingled with the people from this other world, men in evening dress, women in gowns of silk or sequins. Curious eyes glanced at her, a snow-stained waif coming in from the cold, who scarcely seemed to belong here; but she didn't care; she wanted only to get to her room and find Anton.

She entered a world of pink serpentine columns and rich woods, of gold leaf and luxurious carpets in peach and blue and yellow, of chandeliers that dripped glowing crystals. The smell of snow in her nostrils was driven out by the mingled scents of a dozen famous perfume houses. She was trembling with the cold.

And then she saw Anton. Anton and Lavinia Carron, walking through the lobby towards her. His arm was linked in hers. He was wearing evening clothes, she was in a long dress of pearl lamé with her dark hair lifted off her face. They were easily the handsomest couple in the lobby of the Ritz tonight, the king and queen of all these beautiful people.

Gasping for breath, Amy tried to flee, but there were too many people to allow for escape. The press of the crowd brought her up face to face with Anton and Lavinia.

Anton's eyes blazed wide as he saw her. 'Where the hell have you been?' he greeted her savagely.

The shock and the pain of that almost made her legs give way. 'Walking,' she replied.

'Walking? In the snow? Are you insane?'

'I suppose I must be,' Amy replied. Lavinia's violet eyes were mocking, triumphant. How sweet it must be to see her rival, bedraggled and half-frozen, in the lobby of the Ritz!

Anton grasped her arm and half pulled, half led her into an alcove where there was a measure of privacy. Lavinia followed, still smirking.

'You look like death warmed over,' Anton said, lifting Amy's face with a firm grip on her chin and staring into her eyes. 'Why did you run out of the Savoy like that?'

'I had nothing more to say at that point,' she replied, pushing his hand away from her face.

'And now?' Anton demanded in a growl. 'Have you got anything to say now?'

'Not in front of that woman,' Amy retorted, not even deigning to look at Lavinia Carron.

Lavinia's simper faded at the enmity in Amy's tone. 'Are you going to let her talk to me like that, Anton?' she demanded angrily.

'Amy,' Anton said tersely, 'all I need to hear from you is a yes or a no. Is it true or isn't it?'

'I can't talk to you here,' she retorted, 'least of all in front of *her*.'

'She is the one who found out these things about you,' Anton said grimly. 'She is the one who enlightened me. If you want to say anything, then you should be able to say it in her presence.'

'And if you can't understand why I cannot say a word in her presence, then you are not the man I fell in love with,' she retorted through chattering teeth.

'*You* don't love him,' Lavinia hissed, leaning forward with bared teeth. '*You* want to drag him down to your pathetic level. You can offer him nothing except ruin!'

'I do love you, Anton,' Amy said, ignoring Lavinia's outburst. 'The question is, do you love me?'

'I loved someone,' he said heavily, and in the shadows

under his eyes she suddenly saw the pain that he had gone through. 'But I don't know where she is any more.'

'She never existed,' Lavinia said with a brusque laugh. 'Like all these people who appoint themselves custodians of the so-called environment, she liked to pose as a saint, but the truth is something else. Someone who used her pregnancy to blackmail her lover, and then aborted it to get revenge on him, cannot claim any moral high ground! She deserves no consideration whatsoever!'

'And someone with a mind as loathsome as yours should keep her mouth shut,' Amy retorted hotly, acknowledging Lavinia's presence at last. 'How dare you talk about blackmail? Aren't you blackmailing Anton right now? All *you* love is money, Lavinia. You said it yourself in Antibes— nothing else matters to you except lots and lots of money in your bank account.'

Lavinia turned to Anton, her nostrils flaring. 'This is the woman you spent all afternoon scouring London for,' she said harshly. 'She destroyed Martin's happiness. Are you going to let her destroy yours?'

'That's enough from both of you,' Anton said quietly. He glanced at his watch. 'We are due to meet the major shareholders in five minutes. I take it you don't intend to be there, Amy?'

The reception at the Marie Antoinette Suite! She had forgotten all about it. Her snow-soaked clothes weighed heavily on her.

'No,' she replied. 'I can't be there.'

'Do you intend to come to the AGM tomorrow?' he demanded.

'Do you want me there?' she asked, meeting his eyes.

'No,' he said flatly. 'It's probably better if you stay away.'

Amy felt as though her heart was stopping. She could hardly breathe. So it had happened, just as she had always feared it would—had always known it would. Lavinia had won and she had lost. As Lavinia sneered at her now, Amy was unable to even cry.

Anton looked into her eyes one last time. His expression was unfathomable, dark. Then he turned, and, taking Lavinia by the arm, led her towards the Marie Antoinette Suite.

CHAPTER FOURTEEN

THE old house had once seemed so huge to her. Now she saw it as just a simple white cottage with a slate roof and a smoking chimney, nestling among a thicket of birches. The garden, which had once been a terrifying forest through which she had run madly with pounding heart, relentlessly hunted by her enemies, was now revealed as a ragged shrubbery of laburnums, rose bushes and laurels.

But the smell of the house, of wax and wood-fires, was just as she had always remembered it. It filled her with so many memories, some bad, some good, some happy, others irreparably sad.

The heating of the cottage depended on the iron boiler built into the fireplace. It was another cold and snowy morning, and the fire was burning low, so Amy piled more logs into the grate. She nursed the fire until it was blazing and she could hear hot water gurgling through the pipes of the old radiators. The chill began to come off the air.

She went into the kitchen and put on the kettle. While it boiled, she contemplated lunch. For the past few days, her life had been this—concentrating on the simple tasks of making a fire, brewing tea, planning a meal. Nothing more, nothing less. It was about all she could cope with. A broken heart did not allow anything more demanding.

As she washed vegetables, she heard the sound of a car coming up the lane. It was a red family estate, driving slowly and carefully because of the thick snow. She did not recognise it—the cottage had few visitors these days. She watched from the kitchen as the car pulled up next to the

174

garage. A woman and a child got out. The child ran to the cottage. The woman paused to lock the car, then followed.

At last Amy saw who it was—one of the twins, her cousin, Jamie-Lee.

She dried her hands and went to open the door for the visitors. The child, a four-year-old boy named David, jumped into her arms.

'Hi, Aunt Amy!'

'Goodness, you've grown, Davie,' she said, hoisting him in her arms. 'Hello, Jamie-Lee. I've just put the kettle on.'

'It's so warm and cosy in here,' Jamie-Lee said, hauling off her parka and hanging it on the coat rack beside the door. 'You've turned it into a home again.'

'Your dad has gone for a walk down to the village to buy a newspaper and some pipe tobacco,' Amy told her cousin.

'I know,' Jamie-Lee said. 'We saw him as we crossed the bridge. But it's you I wanted to talk to, Amy.'

'OK,' Amy said cheerfully, though a cordial tête-à-tête with her cousin was hardly customary—nor a particularly welcome idea right now. 'I'll pour the tea.'

There were some of the child's toys in a cupboard. Amy got them out so he could play while she and Jamie-Lee sat on either side of the fire. Jamie-Lee was a thin blonde woman with feathery hair. She had married a doctor and lived some two hours' drive away, so she had evidently made a special journey to be here. She seemed nervous, her thin shoulders tense under the expensive cashmere cardigan, her mouth compressed.

'What did you want to talk about?' Amy invited.

Jamie-Lee drew a deep breath. 'I've come to make my peace with you,' she said in a brittle voice. Amy said nothing, cradling the teacup in her hands and watching the flames lick around the logs. Jamie-Lee swallowed and then went on. 'We were loathsome to you, Amy. All three of us. We did and said horrible things to you. When I remember what we were like, I feel sick. You were all alone and you had just lost your parents. You needed us to be kind to you, needed your family to help you, but instead we—'

In the silence, the flames crackled. Still Amy said nothing. It was not her job to help her cousin out with whatever it was she wanted to say.

Jamie-Lee's fingers were shaking and the teacup rattled against the saucer. 'We were talking about it the other day. We were all so ashamed of what we did to you. I know the others want to talk to you themselves, but when I heard you were staying with Dad I decided to come over and apologise to you. I'm so sorry, Amy. More sorry than I can say.'

To her surprise, Amy saw that her cousin's eyes were brimming with tears, her pale lips working painfully. She reached out her hand. 'Don't cry, Jamie-Lee. It was all a long time ago.'

Jamie-Lee put down the cup with a clatter and grasped Amy's hand, sobbing. 'Please say you forgive me,' she begged, 'please say that, Amy.'

'Of course I forgive you,' Amy said, 'though I'll never know why you all disliked me so much.'

Jamie-Lee gave a laugh that was halfway to a sob. 'Oh, of course you know why!'

'I promise you, I don't.'

'Well, because you were so much prettier and cleverer than any of us, of course,' Jamie-Lee said, wiping her eyes. 'You were so talented and we were such mugs. And Dad thought the world of you. You showed us up for what we were.'

'I see,' Amy said quietly.

'And all the boys fancied you like mad—they never even looked at Sally-Ann or me. And then you started winning all those scholarships and bursaries and things. You got honours for sport *and* academics. The teachers adored you, and it was always me or Sally-Ann at the bottom of the pile.

You even started your periods before we did. We were so insanely jealous. And you grew breasts before we did and all the boys were crazier about you than ever—'

'You'd better stop,' Amy said as her cousin's voice rose, 'I don't want you chasing me round the garden with the carving knife again.'

Jamie-Lee gave that half-sob again. 'It's taken me all these years to crawl out from under that inferiority complex, Amy. If it had just been me, I think I would have worshipped you. But there were three of us, you see, and so we ganged up on you. The tall poppy effect, you know. Trying to cut you down to our size. But you just kept growing taller and taller, and the taller you grew, the smaller we felt. When you arrived in our little world, everything turned upside-down. But I finally realised something important.'

'What was that?' Amy asked gently.

'You gave me a wonderful example,' Jamie-Lee said simply. 'I had someone to look up to. I learned from you—to work hard, try my best, to achieve. I wouldn't be the person I am today without you.'

'Well, I hardly—'

'I'm serious,' Jamie-Lee said. 'You're such a good person. So in control of your life. I still envy you like mad, but it's under control now. You have had three wonderful jobs in a row. And now you're in Hong Kong, working for Anton Zell. We're so proud of you; a top job overseas for a wonderful boss, travel, money, excitement—you deserve it so much.'

Amy smiled painfully. 'I'm not so sure it's all it's cracked up to be,' she replied. 'And I don't think I'll be going back to Hong Kong any time soon.' She was feeling shaky. She took the cups back to the kitchen to make fresh tea.

Jamie-Lee followed her. 'What are you talking about?'

'I lost the job.'

'But—why?'

'I concealed some information during the interview process.'

'Professional information? About your qualifications?'

Amy sighed. 'No, something personal. About my private life.'

'But, Amy,' Jamie-Lee protested, 'they're not allowed to bring up your private life during an interview.'

'This job was special.' The last thing she wanted to do was talk about Anton to Jamie-Lee, but her cousin's wide blue eyes were fixed on her. 'The employer was—special. He grew to be special to me, I mean. And I think I did to him.'

'You fell in love with Anton Zell?' Jamie-Lee gasped.

'It's an occupational hazard,' Amy said wryly.

'But—what happened?'

'Things didn't work out.'

'Why?' Jamie-Lee persisted, taking the second cup of tea that Amy gave her.

'Let's just say that perhaps I'm not as good a person as you imagined,' Amy said painfully. 'And I'm certainly not as "in control of my life" as it seems.' She glanced at the little boy playing with toy soldiers on the carpet. 'And you can't envy me a tenth as much as I envy you now,' she finished quietly.

Her uncle returned from his walk just before lunch. He had stayed out longer than usual, probably warned by Jamie-Lee that she wanted time alone with Amy. Retired and grey-haired now, Jeffrey Cookson presented a comfortable figure with his cloth cap and his pipe dangling from under his moustache.

He was carrying a pink newspaper which Amy recognised as the *Financial Times*. He took it from under his arm, unfolded it and passed it to Amy.

'Some news about your boss, my dear,' he said laconically. 'I'm going upstairs to wash.'

Alone by the fire, Amy turned to the article. It was on the front page. The headline read, Zell Buyback Has Impact on Share Prices.

Her heart beating fast, she read the text.

The Zell Corporation's recent buyback of a major block of shares, formerly owned by the late Sir Robert Carron, is now widely perceived to have enhanced shareholder value. ZellCorp share prices surged after news of the buyback was announced at the stormy recent stockholders' meeting.

At the current share price of 134p the dividend yield is 8.9%, and since the dividend appears safe the shares are proving attractive to income investors, though capital growth may be limited as company CEO Anton Zell takes ZellCorp into new areas over the next two years.

Zell denied that the aim of the buyback was simply to give a short-term boost to his company's shares.

'There were differences of opinion on the direction the company should be taking,' he explained, talking from his Hong Kong office. 'In the end, it came down to a crisis of confidence. The simplest solution was for us to buy back blocks owned by dissenting elements. This has proved expensive, especially since our requirement for capital expenditure is set to be high as we expand into new areas. But we now have a free hand to develop the way we want to, and the remaining shareholders have seen the value of their shares substantially increased, which will enhance their confidence in management.'

Lady Lavinia Carron, the principal beneficiary of the buyback, is back in France; however, she made a brief statement today through her financial advisor, Heinz Meyer.

'We disagreed with Mr Zell about his new operations and

on several other fundamental issues. He refused to listen. We got our money back. That's all. The improvement in the share price is immaterial to us. We believe Zell paid too much for his own shares and expect to see a substantial drop in the share price as soon as the public realise their confidence in this man is misplaced.'

Lady Carron received a multimillion-pound cash sum for her shares. However, her prediction that the ZellCorp price is set to fall soon is unlikely to be borne out in reality, as demand for the shares is now very high.

The imminent implementation of exciting new technologies, including advanced recycling refineries and the laminate plate system, has rocketed ZellCorp into the forefront of the petrochemical industry. The market has interpreted the buyback as a highly positive signal from ZellCorp and there is considerable market interest in this company.

The rest of the article dealt with the details of the new technology including a sidebar about the Korean shipbuilding licensing deal, and a photograph of Anton taken at the Ritz during the AGM.

Amy laid down the paper, staring into the flames. Her heart was still thudding. So things had not turned out as she had anticipated. She had been too afraid to read the paper since leaving London. She had simply assumed that Lavinia would carry the day and that Anton would shortly be announcing his engagement to her.

But it hadn't happened that way. The bitterness so evident in Lavinia's Press statement bore out the newspaper's report that the stockholders' meeting had been 'stormy'. She had not, after all, carried the day. Whatever deal she had offered Anton had had no intention of bargaining down his position.

Now Lavinia was back in France and Anton was in Hong Kong. And she was here in Northamptonshire. Their lives had collided passionately and then had gone on their own ways.

Amy rose, restless and agitated, and went into the kitchen. She would give a great deal to have seen Lavinia's performance at the AGM. The venue which she had expected to be the scene of her triumph had turned into her Waterloo.

She would give a great deal, too, to have seen Anton's performance. She had made many mistakes of judgement about Anton Zell. She had assumed that he would let expedience rule his life, the way other men did. But he was not like that.

He was not that kind of man.

She busied herself with preparing lunch for herself and Uncle Jeffrey. But her mind was busy with so many brilliant and fiery images, images of Anton she had locked away until this moment: Anton making love to her, filling her like a sail in a hurricane; Anton making her laugh till she was weak; the deep core of peace she had felt with him as they stood in that temple on an island off the coast of Vietnam.

Her heart filled with tears and restlessness, she laid out the food for her uncle. She sat with him while he ate but could not touch anything herself. Her stomach was in a knot. He did not ask why Jamie-Lee hadn't stayed for lunch, nor about the reason for her visit.

That was his way. Jeffrey had never asked her directly about the reason for her sudden departure from Anton's employment. Perhaps because he was not her real father, he had always kept out of her private life. Yet when she'd needed somewhere to run to, he had asked no questions, had just opened his door to her.

She felt he had always known more than he said about what happened to her, but he did not pry. One day she would be able to explain some of the dark places in her life to him; but not today, not yet.

The snow had stopped falling and the sun was peering

uncertainly through luminous cloud, so after lunch she decided to go for a walk in the woods alone. As a girl, it had always been her refuge, her place to think.

It was early January—almost a year to the day since she had walked into Anton Zell's life, and he into hers.

In the summer, the woods were a deep-dappled place of rustling leaves and teeming bird life. It was strange to walk through them now and see the sky above, criss-crossed with bare twigs, and hear no sound but the crunch of her own boots in the snow.

There was much to think about. It had been such a strange day. Twice in quick succession, her expectations had been transformed. People had behaved as she had never expected they could or would.

She had never anticipated that any of her cousins would ever feel guilty about the wretched childhood they had given her, let alone that she would hear Jamie-Lee, always the ringleader, apologise with tears in her eyes.

And then, the news of Anton's buyback had come as an even greater shock. She knew that Lavinia had seen herself as Anton's consort and could only imagine the huge effort she had made to achieve that goal. Anton could have staved off the crisis by a dozen means. What had happened that awful evening at the Ritz, after she had left, and Anton and Lavinia had walked into the Marie Antoinette Suite together? She would never know.

But somehow, Amy felt that article in the *Financial Times* had rounded off her understanding of Anton; just as Jamie-Lee's apology had rounded off her understanding of her cousins, and had closed the door on a dark and unhappy chapter. Understanding why her cousins had been so resentful of her had helped her understand herself, too.

She had always been such a high achiever, so determined to be at the top, to be the best at everything. Perhaps she too, had been unbearable to them, as they had been to her

But where had it led her, that relentless urge to excel? Into two disastrous experiences. She had become personally involved with two employers in succession. Both relationships had ended in catastrophe.

Hardly the great professional triumph that Jamie-Lee perceived.

And it was painful to see herself through Anton's eyes—as a woman who habitually slept with her bosses, who lied about her past relationships, who concealed what she was under a cloak of hypocrisy.

Of course Martin McCallum would have told Lavinia the story his own way, absolving himself of all blame and making her out to be a monster; and no doubt the story would have improved further as Lavinia relayed it. But the truth was that she had been terribly stupid with Martin and was still paying for it now—would pay for the rest of her life. Because she had lost the one man she had ever loved. The only man she ever could love.

There was a pool at the heart of the wood, fed by a little stream that trickled down from the hills. She reached it late in the afternoon. In happier summers she had swum here, cooling off in the clear water. Today parts of the pool were iced over and its heart was a deep turquoise blue. The sun had set low and was turning crimson through the trees.

Amy sat on a boulder and looked into the aquamarine depths of the pool. It was so still here, in the heart of the woods. Nothing stirred. No creature moved, no wind blew. It seemed to Amy that after so much travel and noise and colour and movement, she had finally reached some still point in her own life—a centre, around which everything else revolved.

In this still place, the decision formed in her heart out of the silence. Retreat and despair were not the answer. She would not accept that it was all over.

She was not that kind of woman.

In this silent moment of her busy life, Amy prayed for the strength to go back to Anton. To find him and tell him the truth about herself. Whatever he decided to do, whatever he chose to believe, she would tell him that she loved him truly and deeply and would never love another man as long as she lived.

She would go back to Hong Kong and look into his eyes once again. Perhaps he would reject her. She would accept that pain if it came. But she would not accept defeat.

She loved him. That was all there was.

The silence was broken by a distant sound, perhaps the cracking of a twig. Amy opened her eyes. She had thought herself alone in the woods. But through the silvery trunks of the trees she could see a figure approaching. It was a tall man, whose outline was so painfully familiar to her that she felt her heart leap into her throat.

Anton stepped into the clearing. Against the muted colours of the snowy woods, his eyes were the deepest blue imaginable, the colour of a warm tropical sea.

'It's almost our anniversary,' he said.

'How did you find me?' she whispered.

'I followed your footprints through the woods,' he replied. 'They were the only ones. Yours are the only footprints in my heart, my beloved Amy. Can you forgive me?'

'Oh, Anton,' she said. She held out her arms and he came to her swiftly.

How wonderful it was to be enveloped in that strong embrace again. She lifted her joyful face to his, accepting his warm kisses with ecstasy, with rapture.

'Please tell me you'll give me another chance,' he begged, crushing her even tighter in his arms. 'Please tell me you forgive me for being such a fool, my beloved.'

'We have both been fools.'

Their kiss seemed to last forever. When the world stopped spinning around them, he looked down into her eyes. 'Yo are the most precious person in my life. Can you pardon me for the terrible words I said to you?'

'If you tell me that you don't believe the things Lavinia told you about me!'

'Not any more. I didn't sleep the night you left, just lay with my own thoughts, realising that it was impossible that the Amy I loved could have done any of that. It was during the meeting itself that it came to me, suddenly, what a madman I had been. I'm so sorry I took so long to find you. You hid yourself well. I had to go straight to Hong Kong after the AGM because of the trouble Lavinia caused. I only got back last night. You know about the buyback?'

She nodded. 'I read about it just this morning. I didn't know before. I just assumed that you and Lavinia—'

'Morticia will have to find another Gomez, my darling.'

She laughed unsteadily. 'She made you pay for rejecting her, my love. I'm sorry about that.'

'It was worth every penny—because now we are free. We can do things our way. And I have some promises to make to you, Amy. One is that our lives will never move at the speed of light again. There will always be time and space for just us. No matter how far we travel, no matter what goals we set ourselves, nothing will matter more than we do. You are the most important person in my world and you always will be.' He kissed her tenderly. 'I will always listen to you and hear the words that you say. Will you come home with me, Amy? Your house is waiting for you, my angel, with dragons to guard all four quarters.'

'You bought Quilin House!'

'Actually, *you* did,' he smiled. 'The house is in your name, beloved.'

'But Anton…why?'

'For one night in London, I thought you didn't exist any more,' he said. 'No night has ever been as dark and terrible as that. Not even when they locked me in the cupboard as a child. When I lost my faith in you, I lost myself. I want to atone for that. I want to show you that I will never again distrust you. I want you to come back to Hong Kong with me and live in your house. It will always be yours, even if you decide not to make me that happiest man in the world and become my wife. But I hope that eventually, you will be ready to marry me. Quilin House is my gift to you, and my apology.'

Another still place, another calm centre, thousands of miles away from that frozen pool.

They stood side by side in the pagoda, holding hands, as they had done once, months before. The ancient shrine was filled with peace. The distant sound of the sea threaded itself around the old stones as though weaving a garland around their blessed happiness. The smile on the face of the statue was serene and beautiful.

As before, they had laid offerings of wild flowers and fruits on the floor of the shrine.

'I never told you how much I loved you,' Anton said. 'If I had done that, perhaps you would have trusted me more.'

'Perhaps I didn't trust myself,' she replied quietly. 'I could never have willingly terminated my pregnancy. But when I had the miscarriage, it seemed to me that it was my fault. I felt such deep guilt for so long. I felt I was to blame somehow.'

His fingers tightened around hers. 'It was an accident of nature,' he replied. 'Only a mind like Martin McCallum's could have believed otherwise.'

'I'm so sorry you had to hear it, warped and twisted like that, from Lavinia. It must have hurt you so terribly.'

'I could never really believe it,' he replied. 'I knew it was wrong, it had to be wrong. You were not the sort of woman who could have behaved in the way she described.' He turned to her, his face serene. 'You are the best and mos beautiful person I know, Amy. I am so proud that you're going to be my wife.'

'And you are the only man in the world,' she replied simply. 'There is no one like you.'

'I've brought something for you,' he said, reaching into his pocket. 'I hope you will accept it this time.'

She knew what it was, even before he held it out to her—a hoop of the deepest, greenest jade, carved with the muscular body of a living dragon.

'The first time I offered it to you,' he went on, 'I think you thought I was trying to mark you as a trophy, a conquest. But I was trying to say the opposite, my love—that you had conquered me, and could wear me on your arm, your own tame dragon.'

'It's so beautiful and alive, just like you. But it will never be tame.' She slipped the cool, precious thing onto her arm and then kissed the warm velvet of his lips. 'I'll never take it off.'

The floor of the temple, as before, was scattered with silvery sand and the flowers that the wind had blown in, as though in mute worship. The domed roof over their heads was filled with the murmur of the sea. Once again, Amy knew that they were in a sacred place, beyond all religion.

'Thank you for bringing me here,' she whispered. 'It's so beautiful.'

'Yes,' Anton replied. 'The world is a beautiful place. I want to spend the rest of my life making sure it stays beautiful for you—and for our children. One of the many reasons I adore you is because you want that, too. I could never love anyone who just didn't care.'

They kissed, with the tenderness of complete love.

Then they turned and walked back down the path, under the drooping boughs of wild hibiscus and ripe fruit that hung like jewels over their heads, back down to the beach, to where their boat was rocking at anchor, waiting to take them onward.

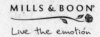

MILLS & BOON®

Live the emotion

Modern
romance™

HIS BRIDE FOR ONE NIGHT by Miranda Lee

Successful divorce lawyer Daniel Bannister didn't believe in love. So why did he meet and marry Charlotte Gale within twenty-four hours? He wanted to have his wedding cake and eat it – and the honeymoon suite was booked and waiting.

SAVAGE AWAKENING by Anne Mather

For two years reporter Matthew Quinn was held captive by rebel forces. Now he's physically scarred. He isn't prepared for Felicity Taylor when she sweeps into his life, and holds back. But his desire for her is strong, and he finds he must confront his past...

THE GREEK'S INNOCENT VIRGIN by Lucy Monroe

Greek tycoon Sebastian Kouros thinks Rachel Long is a scheming money-grabber. The bitterness between them is ripe, and neither is expecting their searing sexual chemistry. Perhaps Sebastian will bed Rachel and then discard her. But Rachel is an innocent...

HIS LIVE-IN MISTRESS by Maggie Cox

Adrian Jacobs needs a housekeeper – but pretty Liadan Willow is not what he has in mind. Liadan finds her new boss intimidating – and magnificently masculine. But does the heat in his eyes mean he wants her in his bed – or in his life?

Don't miss out...

On sale 4th March 2005

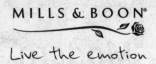

FREE

4 BOOKS AND A SURPRISE GIFT!

We would like to take this opportunity to thank you for reading this Mills & Boon® book by offering you the chance to take FOUR more specially selected titles from the Modern Romance™ series absolutely FREE! We're also making this offer to introduce you to the benefits of the Reader Service™—

- ★ **FREE home delivery**
- ★ **FREE gifts and competitions**
- ★ **FREE monthly Newsletter**
- ★ **Books available before they're in the shops**
- ★ **Exclusive Reader Service offers**

Accepting these FREE books and gift places you under no obligation to buy; you may cancel at any time, even after receiving your free shipment. Simply complete your details below and return the entire page to the address below. You don't even need a stamp!

YES! Please send me 4 free Modern Romance books and a surprise gift. I understand that unless you hear from me, I will receive 6 superb new titles every month for just £2.69 each, postage and packing free. I am under no obligation to purchase any books and may cancel my subscription at any time. The free books and gift will be mine to keep in any case.

P5ZEE

Ms/Mrs/Miss/Mr..Initials ....
BLOCK CAPITALS PLEASE

Surname ....

Address ....

....

....Postcode ....

Send this whole page to:
The Reader Service, FREEPOST CN81, Croydon, CR9 3WZ

Offer valid in UK only and is not available to current Reader Service™ subscribers to this series. Overseas and Eire please write for details. We reserve the right to refuse an application and applicants must be aged 18 years or over. Only one application per household. Terms and prices subject to change without notice. Offer expires 31st May 2005. As a result of this application, you may receive offers from Harlequin Mills & Boon and other carefully selected companies. If you would prefer not to share in this opportunity please write to The Data Manager at PO Box 676, Richmond, TW9 1WU.

Mills & Boon® is a registered trademark owned by Harlequin Mills & Boon Limited.
Modern Romance™ is being used as a trademark. The Reader Service™ is being used as a trademark.

WIN a romantic weekend in PARïS

To celebrate Valentine's Day we are offering you the chance to WIN one of 3 romantic weekend breaks to Paris.

Imagine you're in Paris; strolling down the Champs Elysées, pottering through the Latin Quarter or taking an evening cruise down the Seine. Whatever your mood, Paris has something to offer everyone.

For your chance to make this dream a reality simply enter this prize draw by filling in the entry form below:

Name _____

Address _____

_____Tel no: _____

Closing date for entries is 30th June 2005

Please send your entry to:

**Valentine's Day Prize Draw
PO Box 676, Richmond, Surrey, TW9 1WU**

Terms and Conditions

1. Draw open to all residents of the UK and Eire aged 18 and over. No purchase necessary. To obtain a copy of the entry form please write to the address above. All requests for entry forms from this address must be received by 31st May 2005. One entry per household only. 2. The offer is for one of three prizes of two nights free accommodation in Paris for two adults sharing a twin or double room and based on flights and accommodation being booked as a package. Flights cannot be booked separately or arranged through any other travel company or agent, and are dependent on availability. Holiday must be taken by 31st December 2005. Restrictions on travel may apply. 3. No alternatives to the prize will be offered. 4. Employees and immediate family members of Harlequin Mills & Boon Ltd are not eligible. 5. To be eligible, all entries must be received by 30th June 2005. 6. No responsibility can be accepted for entries that are lost, delayed or damaged in the post. 7. Proof of postage cannot be accepted as proof of delivery. 8. Winners will be determined in a random and independently supervised draw from all eligible entries received. 9. Prize winner notification will be made by letter no later than 14 days after the deadline for entry. 10. If any prize or prize notification is returned as undeliverable, an alternative winner will be drawn from eligible entries. 11. Names of competition winners are available on request. 12. As a result of this application you may receive offers from Harlequin Mills & Boon Ltd. If you do not wish to share in this opportunity, please write to the data manager at the address shown above. 13. Rules available on request.